LELA GRAYCE

Moon Mated

This book was professionally typeset on Reedsy.
Find out more at reedsy.com

Dedicated to Caymen Jack margaritas in the can.
You're my favorite.

Contents

Chapter One	1
Chapter Two	8
Chapter Three	14
Chapter Four	20
Chapter Five	27
Chapter Six	34
Chapter Seven	42
Chapter Eight	48
Chapter Nine	54
Chapter Ten	61
Chapter Eleven	68
Chapter Twelve	74
Chapter Thirteen	81
Chapter Fourteen	88
Chapter Fifteen	96
Chapter Sixteen	102
Chapter Seventeen	109
Chapter Eighteen	115
Chapter Nineteen	122
Chapter Twenty	129
Chapter Twenty-One	139
Chapter Twenty-Two	146
Chapter Twenty-Three	152
Chapter Twenty-Four	158

Chapter Twenty-Five	164
Chapter Twenty-Six	169
Chapter Twenty-Seven	177
Chapter Twenty-Eight	182
Chapter Twenty-Nine	190
Chapter Thirty	194
Moon Forged	195
About the Author	197
Also by Lela Grayce	198

ALPHA SEEKER

BOOK TWO: MOON MATED

LELA GRAYCE

Chapter One

Rylan

Reality was slow to return. The wall between my wolf and me had collapsed with a single touch. I was trapped inside my head with him while my body did Spirit knows what against my will. Feeling returned first but my vision took longer.

My limbs trembled as awareness returned, the present hitting me like a ton of bricks. My right hand was wrapped around the hilt of a blade—a blade that made my skin burn. It was tempered by the fingers I felt on my wrist.

As my sight returned, I recognized the touch. My lips twitched, knowing my mate had saved me from whatever this was. I couldn't wait to show her how appreciative I was later on, but right now I had to assess the situation and figure a way out of this.

Beautiful russet eyes met mine, and I'd know them anywhere. Their depths held my heart and soul, everything that I was and everything I hoped to become.

Red was the next color that registered. For a moment, I thought Pearl had changed her dress. Not that it mattered. She would look stunning in any color or fabric. She could be

1

dressed in a burlap sack, and I'd still want her.

The thought made my blood surge and my pants suddenly become tighter.

A sharp inhale made me shake the rest of the fog off; my body trembled against my will. My eyes sharpened as my wolf merged back with my human side, revealing what exactly I was seeing.

Pearl was in front of me, dressed in the white dress I bought for her, but it wasn't white anymore. It was red. Crimson red bleeding down her front from the blade that was nearly halfway buried in her neck. Right where I was planning my mating bite to go.

Panic gripped my heart, followed swiftly by horror. My hand still held the hilt of the blade that had cut into Pearl's throat.

My other hand was suddenly gripping her shoulder before I made a conscious command for it to move. Her eyes rolled as her body went limp. I caught her before she could drop an inch. I pulled her against my chest, the panic surrounding my heart about to erupt into full blown fight or flight.

That's not what happened. Those instincts were pushed to the side as something dark and visceral bubbled up from deep inside. An energy that burned but also felt incredible.

She's just unconscious from the blood loss.

My jaw clenched as I tried to get a handle on whatever this was, but my wolf stepped in, advising me not to fight it.

Instead, I concentrated on Pearl, on her heartbeat, on her breathing. It didn't help. Every sense I had was filled with my mate, her blood seeping into the material of my tux.

I just got her.

Rage ignited and joined the burning energy that threatened to consume me.

Fur rippled down my arms as my muscles bulged. My body was trying to shift, but my wolf insisted I stay in control. My gums ached as my teeth elongated, cutting my lips and cheeks, the taste of copper coating my tongue.

My head tilted back, a pressure building in my lungs until I couldn't hold it back anymore. A power I'd never felt before and the mightiest roar I could muster met and became something I didn't think I could ever explain.

A sound mixed with so much raw unfiltered anguish and power exploded from every cell in my body. The concussive blast rocked me backward, making me scramble not to drop Pearl since the knife was still lodged in her throat.

"Rylan?" a male voice asked as a presence settled down beside me.

My teeth bared; a warning growl rattled my chest before I realized who it was.

Deacon, my friend.

"I'm here to help," he said, doing his best not to rile me further.

A buzzing filled my ears like a hornet's nest had suddenly decided to take up residence. I fought the urge to shake my head until my wolf forced my attention to the crowd around us.

Shifters from every pack were staring at me while I held my blood-covered mate.

"You broke it. Somehow you broke whatever it was that was controlling everyone."

My attention was on Pearl though. I couldn't care less what happened to everyone else. My mate was all that mattered in this moment. I was ready to say fuck them all. My mate's life wasn't worth this. She deserved so much better than this.

'*Get your shit together, Alpha,*' a depthless voice spoke in my mind sternly.

My wolf bit my tongue before I could respond to the thoughts buzzing in my head.

'*She's not dead. She knew that this wasn't her time. She trusts you to get her out of this.*'

The Moon Spirit was right. I was supposed to unite these people and telling them all to go to hell wasn't what Pearl wanted. Regardless of my current feelings, I couldn't. No matter how much I wanted to put her before the packs.

The very idea made me sick to my stomach, but I pushed it all aside. Right now, I needed to get my head straight, and I needed to keep skin-to-skin contact with Pearl. Otherwise, I would be susceptible to whatever control Tamra was using.

This posed a different problem. I couldn't fight and maintain contact with Pearl. What I needed to do was get us out of this situation and regroup. We'd fight another day.

"Look out!" Deacon yelled, moving to put himself between me and the assailant.

A snarling growl ripped through the silence, followed by a scream of pain.

"Holy shit!" Deacon exclaimed, watching the scene with wide eyes.

I turned my head as far as I could without dislodging Pearl. A white wolf was growling and shaking my aunt Tamra's arm. She screamed as blood dripped from the wound, staining the muzzle of the wolf crimson.

Confused, I glanced around and found the Moon Spirit sitting beside me watching the commotion with dark blue eyes that saw more than I ever could.

'*She's been waiting for this for a long time,*' the Moon Spirit whispered in my thoughts, eyes flicking to mine quickly. *'I couldn't tell her no.'*

I nodded, pretending that I understood.

"Enough!" my aunt roared, drawing my attention back to the fight.

Tamra had managed to shake off the wolf and was now cradling her mangled arm. Her eyes were wide as she stared at the red stained wolf, her face going pale. The two stared at each other for several heartbeats, the kind of look that held a whole conversation.

The wolf's hackles rose, revealing fangs covered in sticky blood and saliva. This seemed to shake my aunt out of a daze. She looked around the room like she forgot what she had been doing until her eyes landed on me and the Moon Spirit sitting by me.

"Ah, I remember now." My aunt smiled, and in that moment, I realized that she wasn't my aunt at all. She was something different. I felt the presence of enormous power coming from her. A darkness that called to me seductively.

It felt familiar, like I'd felt this before. My wolf moved my hand, so my skin was pressed against Pearl's. I wasn't sure what it meant, but my mind remained clear and sharp as long as I stayed in physical contact with her.

A surge of energy rocked me, followed by a blast that I felt more than heard. The Moon Spirit's chest began to rumble with a growl as the blanket of force settled over everyone in the room.

Together, in perfect synchronization, every shifter took a step forward and spoke like they were all one collective being.

"You have no power here."

'I think that's our cue. We need to regroup.' Deacon's hand was

on my shoulder, and I realized his mind was clear. I guess contact with me had the same effect that Pearl had on me.

"We can't stay here," I spoke quietly. The wolf beside me nodded minutely while the hand on my shoulder squeezed, letting me know I'd been heard.

"I know a place," he replied just as softly. "A safe house."

I'll cause a distraction. Estella will join you,' the Moon Spirit said, moving to a standing position.

I looked toward the head of the room to the alpha table. My uncle and cousin stood amongst the others, looking dazed, and I knew that whatever had happened to me was now happening to them. They were trapped inside themselves, and I didn't think I had the strength or knew how to break the enchantment again.

"Keep your hand on me at all times," I told Deacon, hoping he realized just how lucky he was not to be trapped like so many others.

"Got it." Deacon squeezed my shoulder again.

The bloody wolf backed up until it was next to the Moon Spirit.

A sharp and shrill whistling split the air before part of the building exploded. I covered Pearl as best as I could while avoiding pieces of the roof raining down on the gathered crowd.

"Keep moving," Deacon advised, pushing bystander statues aside. I prayed that they regained control of themselves.

'They will, eventually,' the Moon Spirit spoke in my mind, sadness clear in its voice.

"What was that thing?" I asked, not expecting an answer but needing to say it out loud.

"No idea, but it was big," Deacon answered, clearly fighting back the shock.

'It was a heavenly body.'

What the fuck is that?

The Moon Spirit chuckled, the answer sounded eerie as it echoed in my thoughts, sending a chill down my spine. *'A meteor.*

Chapter Two

Pearl

I was floating in liquid warmth that was thicker than water. I thought for a moment that it was blood. I panicked sucking in a breath, not detecting a smell.

I sighed then relaxed, letting my arms float beside me. I felt no pain, only calm.

"It's lovely, isn't it?" a female voice asked, startling me.

I tried to sit up, but I only managed to dunk my head below the surface. A tinkling laughter echoed around me as I rose to standing, sputtering.

"It's not deep," the voice said, the tone grating on my nerves.

My eyes stung from a light that was pure and blinding.

"Where am I?" I wondered, looking around at the peaceful pool I stood in.

"This is the Between," the woman whispered, sounding like she was standing right next to me. "This is the place that souls go when they are neither dead nor alive."

Dead?

The word rang inside my head, resonating like a gong. I shook my head, trying to remember why that word felt like a stab in the heart.

"Part of us is still alive," the voice reassured.

I whipped around, trying to pinpoint where the voice was coming from.

"Who are you?" I turned in a circle but saw nothing other than the shimmering surface of the pool.

"Don't be afraid."

I spun and came nose to nose with a woman. Her skin was so smooth that it couldn't be real, maybe a mirage. Except, her hair was darker, hanging in perfect ringlets that framed her face. She looked to be about my age, though her ocean-blue eyes seemed much older.

"What's your name?" I asked, not reacting to her nakedness since I was naked too.

"Estella." She smiled at me. "What's your name?"

I opened my mouth to respond then closed it, trying to recall what my name was. Something white and iridescent flashed through my thoughts, making me pause and consider what it could mean.

"Looks like a Pearl," Estella commented, as if she reached out and plucked it from my mind.

"Pearl?"

It sounded like a name—a pretty one for something precious. There was more, I could feel it in my head, but no matter how hard I tried, I couldn't access it.

A stab of pain spiked through my skull. I cried out, and Estella reached forward and steadied me.

"Are you alright?"

No! I wanted to scream but bit my tongue. I got the feeling that Estella was fragile. She'd obviously been here a long time.

"How long have you been here?" I asked instead.

"A while." She frowned as she considered my question. "I'm

not entirely sure."

Alarm bells rang in the back of my mind. She seemed genuine, but I couldn't help but think that I knew her. That was impossible since I had just met her. I returned her frown.

"How long have I been here?" I looked around at the expanse of liquid that filled the space.

Above me was brightness but nothing more. I considered what Estella had called this place. The Between. She'd said that being here meant we were neither alive nor dead, which would be impossible, but I couldn't get my brain fog to clear enough to ask why or even how. Being here was a mystery. The answers had to be in my head. If I could just remember what happened before I got here.

Instinctively, I reached for a presence in my mind, but there was nothing. I was completely alone inside my own head. My heart sped up as that discovery made me panic, but I wasn't sure why. All I knew was that being alone inside my head was bad. I got the feeling that I had never really been alone.

"You haven't been here long." Estella watched me with her unnerving eyes and smooth countenance.

Was she even real? I reached my hand out and touched her shoulder. Her skin felt as smooth as it looked, plus she was solid, which meant she was real or as real as one could be in this place.

"You said we are neither alive nor dead, so what exactly are we?"

"The Moon Spirit brought us here for safe keeping. This is its domain."

The Moon Spirit? Who the hell was....

An image popped into my head of a white wolf that seemed to glow with ethereal power. Its dark blue eyes stared at me, and I silently begged it to help me remember.

Pearl?

The name startled me, but the voice was different. It wasn't Estella's but deep and masculine. It made my knees weak and my heart long for whomever the speaker was. I followed the thought, diving down deep into my subconscious.

Green-gray eyes appeared, and I recognized them. The gray was the man, and the green represented something else. Depending on the mood, the colors would deepen. A strong jawline with stubble tickled my palm every time I touched it. He had dark hair that I loved to run my fingers through while breathing in his scent and imprinting it on my soul.

Rylan.

The name jumped to the forefront of my mind, making my stomach lurch. How could I have forgotten him?

'You haven't forgotten him,' a voice said kindly in my head.

'He's my mate.' I desperately wished I was with him right now instead of trapped here.

'You aren't trapped here,' the voice corrected, pulling up a memory and showing it to me. *'You were injured badly. Your body is healing, supervised by your wolf and mate. You'll be able to return soon.'*

Tears pricked my eyes as I imagined Rylan hovering over my broken body, probably beating himself up for letting me get hurt. I didn't blame him. It had happened while saving him. I'd do it all over again if given the choice.

'Why did you bring me here?' I wanted nothing more than to return to my body, to my mate.

'It was the safest place to put your soul, plus I wanted you to meet Estella.'

I looked back at the naked girl I was still holding onto. Her lips lifted into a small smile, and a feeling of déjà vu came over me. I had met her before, sort of. I met her wolf. The white one who I kept mistaking for the Moon Spirit.

"It's you," I whispered, looking her over again with new eyes. "What are you doing here?" Her wolf wasn't here with her, which seemed strange.

'Estella is the reason I sent you here.'

I looked at her and noticed tears swimming in her eyes as the Moon Spirit spoke to both of us. She had been stuck here for who knew how long without her wolf in this place of limbo.

'How do we get out of here?' I mentally asked the Moon Spirit.

'I can bring you back, but I need your help in return.'

'Help with what?'

'I can't bring Estella back by myself. I need your help.'

'Of course. Whatever I need to do.'

I couldn't imagine being separated from my wolf for any amount of time. Now that I'd experienced it, I swore to myself that I would never take being with my wolf for granted again.

My thoughts turned to Rylan and what he must be thinking and feeling. I hoped he knew that none of this was his fault, but knowing him, he probably blamed himself.

'He needs you, Pearl.'

I need him.

Tears pricked my eyes, and an overwhelming desire to get back to him came over me. My breathing became labored, and stars danced in my periphery.

'What do I need to do?' I asked the Moon Spirit, turning to see its white wolf standing on top of the water.

'This won't be pleasant,' the wolf warned, hackles rising in a snarl to show off its impressive canines.

I swallowed thickly before straightening my shoulders. I'd

do whatever it took to get back to Rylan and bring Estella with me.

Chapter Three

Rylan

I didn't expect much since we were technically on the run from all the packs now, but a small, secluded cabin on the very edge of pack lands wasn't what I had in mind.

The Moon Spirit had disappeared halfway into our run to this place. The path wasn't exactly a straight line either. Deacon backtracked and did every trick in the book to cover our tracks.

All of *my* attention was too focused on Pearl's nearly nonexistent heartbeat to offer to erase our scents.

The white wolf, Estella, kept pace with me, running like she did this every day. Her bottom jaw and chest were covered in blood, making her look savage. I wasn't sure why she didn't shift to her human form, but maybe she just didn't want to. I could respect that.

Deacon opened the door like he owned the place, and I beelined for the first cushioned surface I could find. The couch was old and the fabric soft from years of wear, which told me this place had been well used.

I placed Pearl gently on the cushions, careful not to dislodge the blade still in her throat. The sight of it and the red-stained white dress made my hands tremble.

Seeing my mate in this state had my control hanging on by a thread. I wanted to get my hands on my aunt and wring her fucking neck. I still wasn't entirely sure what had happened, but coming back to oneself only to see a blade they held buried in the neck of their mate would make any wolf go crazy.

"I'll get some bandages," Deacon offered before hurrying off somewhere.

I sank to my knees so my face was on the same level as hers. The wound looked red and angry, making my heart lurch, thinking she'd gotten an infection, which was unheard of for shifter kind. Her breathing was shallow and far apart and I knew the end was close.

What have I done?

"Rylan?" Deacon asked, back in the room with a rustle of fabric.

"This is my fault," I whispered, fists clenched as wave after wave of emotion crashed over me until I was vibrating.

A cold nose nudged my arm, startling me out of my emotional spiral. I drew back, thinking the wolf wanted to pay her last respects. Instead, her canines bit the handle of the blade.

I reacted on instinct, grabbing the wolf by the throat, but a quick jerk of her head dislodged the knife. A roar escaped me as I threw Estella across the room, blade still in her mouth.

The smell of fresh blood distracted my murderous intentions. I turned back to Pearl, expecting the wound to be gushing and for her to take her final breath.

A small trickle of crimson spilled from the cut. Not the amount I was expecting. I stepped closer, eyes trained on my mate's neck, surprised to find it looking better with every second that passed.

"The blade was blocking her healing ability," Deacon said, eyes wide as he too studied Pearl's neck.

"It looks better, but her heart rate and breathing are nonexistent."

Physically, she was healing, but her insides didn't seem to be.

"She lost a lot of blood. It'll take time for things to return to normal," Deacon spoke softly, laying a gentle hand on my shoulder.

"What happened?" I hoped he knew what I was referring to.

"I remember being trapped inside my head, unable to reach my wolf or my body. It was horrible." He swallowed, eyes looking disturbed and frightened. "After what seemed like forever, a wave of unimaginable power washed over me. Whatever that power was destroyed the barriers in my mind, making me whole again."

I remembered that feeling, but instead of power, it was my mates' touch that demolished the cage I was trapped in.

Estella walked around the couch like she was trying to shake off the impact.

"I'm sorry," I said, ready to explain that I was on edge and not in full control.

She huffed, like she knew removing the blade would cause a reaction from me. She'd been expecting something, no doubt, which was dangerous because I could have easily killed her.

Her wolf eyes met mine, and I could see the enormous amount of pain in them. She understood my agony, but I had no idea what caused hers.

I nodded, and she and I appeared to come to some sort of mutual understanding. We each felt the bitter sting of helplessness as we stood by and watched the people we cared about in pain, and we could do nothing to help them.

16

'You can help. Right here, right now.' The Moon Spirit's voice sounded urgent in my head. *'You can help your mate and Estella by doing exactly as I say.'*

'Name it,' I replied frantically. Ready for whatever needs to be done.

'I have your mate and Estella, but they cannot return without assistance.'

"Whatever it is, I'll do it!" I spoke out loud, needing to say the words full of frustration and compliance.

'Calm down. I need you to be levelheaded to do this.'

I took a deep breath, doing my best to calm my racing heart. If calm and focused was what I needed to be, then I'd do it. For Pearl.

"Tell me what I need to do."

'Close your eyes and reach for the connection you have to Pearl. Reach through it until you can feel her, then grab her and guide her back.'

'Back where?' my wolf asked, but I ignored him and instead turned his and my attention to the newly created bond with our mate.

I closed my eyes, pushing away all distractions, including Deacon, who was currently yelling at me. It didn't matter. The only thing that mattered was getting Pearl.

Darkness greeted me, followed by my wolf. He turned and trotted away. Since he was better at dealing with bonds, I let him lead.

It felt weird to race after my wolf in my mind, but I continued on, believing what the Moon Spirit had said. Wherever Pearl was, she needed our help to return, and I wouldn't question that. Ever.

A small spark of silvery-white light appeared in the absolute darkness. Once I saw it, I knew it had to be where Pearl was. Together, my wolf and I rushed toward the speck of light, watching as it grows larger the farther we sprinted.

After an eternity of running in darkness, the light finally filled the space. We slowed our pace as the close proximity revealed a human-like shape standing in front.

'Pearl?' I reached for her in reflex.

'Rylan,' she replied, a smile spreading across her face when she saw me.

She took my hand, and the touch was one I could feel in my very soul. I tried to pull her closer, but I couldn't.

'What now?' I asked her, doing my best not to let my emotions get out of control.

'You need to guide me back.' She squeezed my hand in reassurance.

'All right.' I turned and faced the way we'd come, the darkness nearly oppressive in contrast to the brilliant light that followed my mate everywhere.

My wolf stood beside me, ready to guide our mate back to reality. I took a step forward, expecting Pearl to come with me, but she didn't. I glanced over my shoulder wondering what the holdup was, but I just saw Pearl with her arm outstretched.

I frowned, looking down at our joined hands then up to her face again.

'I know I said guide,' Pearl said, sheepishly shifting her weight from foot to foot, 'but you may need to put in more effort than that.'

What did that mean?

'Do I need to pull you?' I asked her.

'I think so.' She appeared uncertain then glancing at the light behind her.

18

I stepped closer to her, my eyes catching hers, and I did my best to relay through them that I had this. She could trust me. I'd do anything to get her back safely.

Her lips quivered slightly, but the smile remained on her face.

'Let's try again.' I turned around once more, staring into the blackness and straightening my shoulders. My wolf rubbed against me, reminding me that he was here. The reminder helped relieve the tension in my chest.

I took a step forward then another. My arm was stretched backward, fully extended as I imagined hers was as well.

With the next step, I pulled on my mate's wrist gently at first before adding more pressure until I felt her resistance break. She took a step forward, the tremble in her arm unmistakable. I wasn't sure if this was her trepidation or if this much resistance was normal.

Regardless, I had to lead her through my mind that I was embarrassed for her to see. This was more intimate than sex, and I was afraid she'd somehow find me lacking. The darkness in my mind was absolute, with only the light from my mate piercing its black depths.

What would her light reveal?

Chapter Four

P earl

Navigating through Rylan's mind was an experience.

It wasn't pleasant or terrible, just dark and full of foreboding. I couldn't figure out why it was like this. Reuniting with me should have been a happy occurrence, but it didn't feel like that.

The light behind me illuminated the space around us, and while the shadows roiled and shifted, I couldn't make out distinct shapes.

Rylan didn't look back or side to side, just straight ahead with his wolf keeping pace beside him. It was strange to see the two of them at the same time, but it also felt natural. Like this was how they always were.

I squeezed Rylan's fingers, hoping to reassure him that I was all right. Something more was going on though.

Finally, we were standing in a dimly lit area that seemed well used, which was probably his regular headspace.

Rylan turned, eyes flicking to the light behind me before meeting my eyes. I wondered if he could feel the presence of another in it. Telling him would lead to more questions which would waste time that we didn't have.

'*What now?*' he asked, his wolf tilting his head like he was confused.

'*Return to yourself, then command me back.*'

'*Command you?*' His eyebrows scrunched adorably, like they always did when he didn't understand.

'*You are* the *alpha. Your command demands obedience.*'

I expected him to argue or maybe question what I was talking about, but instead he took a breath and nodded.

He tried to drop my hand, but neither one of us could break the connection. His lips pulled down into a frown before he lowered his gaze to his wolf, its eyes sparkled like he knew something Rylan didn't.

Pulling me closer, Rylan stretched my hand toward his wolf. As soon as my skin made contact with his wolf's fur, he was able to release my hand.

I smiled at the wolf before looking up at my mate, and the arms I was dying to return to. His jaw was clenched, but I couldn't make out what he was feeling. In the next second, he was gone, leaving me with his wolf, who seemed incredibly eager to be alone with me.

'*He blames himself,*' the sock-footed wolf revealed, speaking into my mind.

'*How are we able to speak to each other?*' I wondered, not that I didn't want to get to know his wolf.

'*Pulling you through our mind also pulled the mate bond closer. Making it more solid.*'

'*So, the bond is in here?*'

'*In here? Yes. Once outside, we won't have this contact until the mating is complete.*'

The reminder of the mating sent a shiver of anticipation down my spine. I wasn't a horn dog normally, but now that

I'd had a taste of my mate, I couldn't seem to get enough.

'We feel the same.'

If I was in my body, I would be blushing scarlet, but here inside of Rylan's mind, there was no embarrassment. Just understanding and acceptance.

"Pearl." My name echoed in the space.

The words brought memories of me to the forefront of Rylan's mind. They played around me like little projections. My face flashed in every direction, and for several moments, I got to see what I looked like through my mate's eyes.

"Pearl!" This time, my name was called with more emotion.

I could feel his worry about me in that one word. Rylan had seemed emotionless guiding me through himself, but those emotions weren't being suppressed any longer.

'What does it mean?' I wondered, unaware that I had directed the question at Rylan's wolf.

'Coming back to himself to see his hand holding the blade that was lodged in your throat...' The wolf growled, like he couldn't help himself. *'It messed with both of us.'*

'You said he blames himself?'

'Yes, but he won't listen to me.' The wolf shrugged, and I had to suppress a laugh. He seemed to feel the way I did about his human half—exasperated.

"Pearl... please."

Those softly spoken words hurt my heart. I sensed his regret, but what he didn't know was that I didn't blame him in the slightest. Seeing that I forgave him for his part in this, maybe he could forgive himself.

The desire to tell him, to make him see how much I needed him was just what needed to happen. Darkness closed around my vision. I was weightless, but with the Moon Spirit's

22

presence all around me, I knew that I was in good hands.

I settled into my body, feeling strange but also relieved that I was back where I belonged. I took stock of my body and found that I was whole again with no pain in my neck. Or anywhere, really.

My eyes opened, and Rylan's face was the first thing I saw. Eyes the color of a summer storm, with a hint of green that was his wolf. I had a new appreciation for his irises. Ones that I could read a little better after being in his mind.

I smiled, my heart leaping to find myself returned to my body and here with him.

"I'm back," I announced out loud. My wolf huffed in my head, but I could sense her relief.

I gave her a mental hug, promising that we would go for a run the first chance we got. She agreed then let me turn my attention to what was happening in the room.

Estella's white wolf was whimpering. I thought that maybe she was in pain until I realized that it was just the wolf.

"Shit!" I exclaimed, sitting up and throwing myself off the couch.

Rylan grabbed me, but I shook him off, crawling until I was face to face with the white wolf. Her body trembled fiercely while her eyes rolled around in their sockets.

"Shh, it's okay," I said, trying to soothe her, but I knew she'd waited years for this. "Rylan, I promise I'll explain later, but right now I need you to say her name. Like you did mine."

I was facing the wolf, but I could feel the danger he posed at my back. My first instinct was to turn toward him, but I couldn't look away from the distressed wolf in front of me.

"Estella," Rylan said, his voice deeper than usual.

"With feeling, like you're calling her," I instructed, hoping that was what was needed in order for her to return.

"Estella," Rylan called again, voice even deeper than it was before.

A flash entered my mind, reminding me of the light that I'd traveled through Rylan's mind with.

"The light, Rylan. Picture the light." The trembling in Estella's wolf had steadily gotten worse, until she was vibrating under my hands. "Hurry!"

"Estella!" Rylan roared, his voice a command that rattled me to my very bones.

A light flashed, illuminating the space we were in, forcing my eyes to shut. As soon as it faded from behind my eyelids, I flicked them open, meeting the gaze of her wolf.

A body was curled on the floor at the wolf's feet. I recognized the dark hair that mixed with the white wolf's fur.

I sighed in relief, happy beyond words that this worked. Tears filled my eyes as I looked up at Rylan, who now stood closer with a confused look on his face.

"Thank you," I whispered, grabbing his hand as tears streamed down my cheeks.

"What the hell just happened?" a male voice asked, drawing my attention.

"This is Deacon, my friend," Rylan hurriedly introduced, tripping over the word friend, making me frown. "I'd also like to know what happened."

I launched into an explanation of the Between, that I was sent there so my body could heal, and so I could meet someone. With the Moon Spirit's help, we devised a plan to get us both back.

"It had to be *the* alpha," I revealed, turning to Rylan and smiling. "Only the true alpha could call us back from the

Between."

"I didn't know I could do that?" He looked shocked at the revelation.

"That doesn't explain who she is," Deacon pointed out, raising his hands in surrender when the white wolf growled at him.

"This wolf and the human are the same." It was the simplest way to explain it, but I knew it wasn't nearly enough. "This is Estella, and this is Estella." I pointed to the girl then the wolf. "The same, just in different forms."

"Why is she like that?" Rylan looked over both.

"I don't know, but the human side has been stuck in the Between for years, separated from her wolf."

"I've never heard of a shifter being split into two different forms." Deacon was staring at them, curiosity clear in his eyes.

"Neither have I," Rylan added, frowning as he tried to make sense of what I was saying and what he was seeing.

"The Moon Spirit wanted them reunited."

"Are they stuck like this?" Rylan glanced at me, like I had all the answers.

"I don't know. The Moon Spirit tasked me to return with her. Beyond that, I'm just as lost as you are."

"Well, let's take her somewhere more comfortable," Deacon stepped toward the two versions of Estella while Rylan lifted me up and out of the way.

The white wolf growled; a low sound full of menace that spoke volumes to everyone in earshot.

"I just want to help," Deacon assured her, gathering the human in his arms before standing and carrying her down a hallway, where I assumed the bedrooms were.

"Where are we?" I took in the unfamiliar room.

"Some place safe." Rylan avoided my eyes.

"Rylan..."

I reached for him, but he backed away, looking at everything but me. I frowned. I thought he'd be happy to see me, but I was getting the cold shoulder.

What the fuck?

His wolf had warned me that he was in a mood, but the silent treatment wasn't what I expected. Was he upset with me?

Without warning, emotions flooded through me, making my lungs seize as I fought the overwhelming feelings. I glanced down at my hands, hoping to distract myself from the wave building inside, but crimson drew my attention.

My once white dress was now stained red. I swallowed, staring at the dried blood that coated me from my neck to my feet.

The amount was staggering, and my knees weakened at the sight while my stomach twisted.

I was coated in my near death, and that realization sent me over edge. Before I could fully collapse, hands grabbed me and lifted me into strong arms. My head spun and darkness descended, closing me into an embrace that I was happy to escape into.

Chapter Five

Rylan

I swung Pearl up into my arms, her limp form nearly sending me into a spiral, but somehow, I held it together. Her scent filtered through my nose, and I felt slightly calmer. She was here. She was safe in my arms, and I wouldn't allow anything else to happen to her.

But you did. A dark voice whispered in the far recesses of my mind. I tried not to listen; I couldn't help but feel that the words were right. I was the one who held the knife as it sliced into my mate's neck. I had no memory of it, however there was no denying it was me.

'She doesn't blame us,' my wolf said, trying to reassure me.

It didn't. I was so wound up that I didn't know how I was going to relieve the pressure and shame flooding me.

Pearl's dried blood flaked off her skin, and I had the sudden urge to wipe it away. Turning, I walked along the opposite hallway that Deacon had disappeared down. I kicked open the first door I came to, glad to find a spacious bedroom.

I carried my mate toward the attached bathroom, shutting the door once inside. There was a tub and separate shower with glass doors. I paused for a moment, debating which one

I should use, but the thought of Pearl leaving my arms was something I wasn't ready to for.

The lid to the toilet was closed, so I carefully perched my mate on it to quickly undress and start the shower. Returning, I tried for a moment to unzip the white dress, but the massive blood stain made my hands shake in anger. I grabbed the fabric and tore the gown from my mate's body.

The motion roused Pearl; her beautiful eyes fluttered open. I pulled the dress off and then gathered her into my arms once more.

I stepped into the shower, standing under the stream of water so it wouldn't hit her directly. The warmth helped me relax and focus on what needed to be done in the moment. Carefully, I deposited Pearl onto a bench, grabbed a bottle of soap, and poured some into my hands.

My mate didn't protest as I washed her body, running over her skin, gently removing the dried blood. Doing this eased my nerves further, until all I could think about was the fact that she no longer smelled of copper. She smelled like rain with an undertone of me. My wolf growled in my head, happy that our mate was starting to smell like us.

I rinsed the suds from her body, following the stream with my hands, a reassuring motion that proved she was all right. Once done, I replaced the shower head, sat beside her then wrapped my arms around her, nestling my nose against her throat where the knife had been buried.

"I'm so sorry," I whispered, placing gentle kisses over her skin.

"I don't blame you." Pearl sighed and relaxed in my embrace. "I'm just glad you're okay."

I pushed back, needing to see her face, to look into her eyes

28

and reassure myself that she was alive. The memory of her slow heartbeat was enough to make rage flit across my mind. Pearl's hands cupped my cheeks, her thumbs sweeping over my skin almost hypnotically.

"I don't know what I'd do if something happened to you." My words were soft but full of fear. This couldn't...no this *wouldn't* happen again. I'd make sure of it.

"I feel the same way. It's not your fault."

I wanted to believe her, but the gut-wrenching fear I had seeing her covered in blood because of the blade I held was something I wouldn't be forgetting anytime soon. She may not blame me, but I sure did. I needed to be stronger.

Pearl leaned forward, brushing her lips against mine. The light touch sparked a fire inside me. I buried my hands in her wet hair, devouring her mouth, determined to imprint the taste of her in my memories. She returned everything I gave, plundering my mouth in equal raptor. Her hands ran over my shoulders, back, and chest. I grew harder the more she touched me, feeling like she was stroking my dick instead.

A self-satisfied growl rumbled through my chest when she moaned my name, her legs straddled me wrapping around my waist, encouraging me closer. My body ached to bury myself inside her, to feel her everywhere and bind her to me. It was selfish to be thinking of mating right now, but I couldn't help the desire. I wanted Pearl in every way possible, so much so that it was almost painful.

I broke the kiss, pressing my forehead to hers and taking some deep breaths to calm the raging lust I felt. She had just been through something traumatic; the last thing she needed was a horny mate who couldn't control his urges.

Reaching up, I turned the water off, forcing myself to stand

and exit the shower in search of towels. I grabbed a stack of them and placed them on the floor by the glass door. Stepping back in, I took Pearl's hands and helped her to her feet then led her out.

I wrapped a towel around her torso and did my best to wrap the other one around her silky moon-white hair, making her giggle at my attempt. Toweling myself off quickly, I took hers to finish drying her. It felt strange, but I couldn't fight the urge to do everything myself.

Once dry, I picked her up again, carried her back into the room and sat her down on the bed. I dug through the closet and dresser, finding a couple pairs of boxers and oversized t-shirts. It would have to do until I could get us our own stuff.

"Rylan?" Pearl asked quietly, her brown eyes watching as I helped her dress.

"Hmm?"

"What happened? How did you escape?"

I bristled at the question; my jaw clamped down so hard I thought my teeth might shatter. I took a deep breath, then another, the earlier spark of anger raging through my mind. I was drowning in anger, fear, and despair when Pearl's hand touched my face. The contact made all of the negative emotions fade away. I took another deep breath, covering her hand with my own.

"I regained control just in time to catch you when you collapsed," I began, swallowing my trepidation. She deserved to know what happened, and while the thought of reliving everything made my stomach churn, I'd promised myself I would never lie to her.

I told her everything that happened after I caught her, including the explosion from the meteor. The destruction

30

was the opening the Moon Spirit had provided in order for us to get out of there.

"Deacon led the way while I carried you, and Estella ran beside me."

"Who's Deacon?" Pearl asked, making me grin.

"He is the alpha-apparent for the Sanda pack," I answered, warmed by her question. "I met him while I was away, and we became fast friends."

"That's awesome!" Pearl clapped her hands excitedly which made me smile. Making friends was always difficult for me. My theory was that on an instinctual level other wolves could tell I was powerful.

"No more excitement. You need to rest." I grabbed and pulled the covers back and slipped between the sheets.

A wicked smile spread across her face that made my stomach muscles clench. She was absolutely perfect. Love filled me up as she settled in beside me, her eyes full of contentment. It made my chest swell. As her mate, it was incredible to know that beside me was the only place she wanted to be.

I tossed the covers over the both of us, expecting her to calm down and rest after the ordeal she'd been through. Instead, her leg was tossed over my hips, I grabbed her thigh instinctively, unprepared for her next actions.

She leaned over me, lips pressing to mine as she pulled herself sideways until she was straddling me fully. I groaned when her fingers teased the skin just beneath the hem of my boxers. My whole body tensed under her touch as she teased and explored, making my eyes roll when her fingers came dangerously close to my erection. I was primed and ready to make her mine in every way.

"Wait." I grasped her shoulders and breathed heavily. "I don't think this is the right time."

"What do you mean?" Pearl frowned, then rocked her hips.

I bit my lip. "We've both been through something traumatic; let's not rush into anything."

"But I want this." She pouted, looking so damn cute that I almost gave in.

"I do too," I assured her, pushing my hips up into her so she could feel the effect she had on me. "I want nothing more than to make you mine." I sat up, wrapping my arms around her, my lips caressing hers until she was gasping and grinding against me.

"Please," she begged, causing my arousal to kick up a notch and my wolf to push forward, ready to give her whatever she wanted.

My mouth caught her nipple, my tongue teasing the bud through her shirt. Her sighs and moans spurred me on. I nipped gently and tugged, making her cry out in ecstasy.

"Fuck." I groaned, pulling the waistband of her boxers down then off her legs.

She settled on me once more, her wetness and arousal teasing my erection. She rocked against me, and her clit caught on the head cock, making my head spin.

This wasn't right. We couldn't do this.

Pearl deserved to be worshiped, to have the mating she'd always dreamed of. It was my duty to make that happen.

Gritting my teeth and fighting my own desires, I slipped my hand between Pearl's legs, replacing my dick with my fingers. I pushed into her, finding the spot that drove her crazy and letting her buck and ride me until she was screaming. She threw her head back, her wet white hair cascading down around her. She looked like a goddess, with her cheeks flushed

32

and my fingers buried inside of her.

She rolled off me, breathing heavily as she recovered from the orgasm that was still taking up space in my mind. Every time we were together, I could feel our bond strengthening, sharing more between us. I pulled her to me—her back against my front and my arm wrapped securely around her.

It took a long time after Pearl fell asleep for me to drift off. Every little noise from the unfamiliar house was an enemy hellbent on taking what was mine. That wasn't going to happen. It had been a close call earlier, one that wouldn't be happening again.

Exhaustion pulled me into slumber, but I vowed silently to myself and Pearl that I wouldn't allow her to be in a position like that again. If I had to shackle her to me to keep her safe... well that was just what I was going to do.

Chapter Six

Pearl

I woke up tired and confused. Last night didn't go as I expected, and I didn't mean the almost dying part. Somehow, Rylan and I had gotten out of sync, or he wasn't getting the hints I was dropping. I just didn't think I'd have to spell it out, but maybe I did.

Rylan was pressed against my back, his hand resting firmly on my thigh just below my hip. It was deliciously distracting. I'd craved his touch before, but somehow, it had ramped up since I came back from the Between. I didn't just crave it now; I needed it. The bond between us had gotten stronger, the pull I felt to him undeniable and hard to resist. The urge to complete the mate bond was a constant throbbing between my thighs.

While I wanted nothing more than for Rylan to distract me with his body, I couldn't deny that it wasn't the right time or place. Yet, a part of me was restless, needing the mate bond to be complete so I could focus on other things.

There was no other way. I had to tell Rylan what I was feeling. As my mate I had to trust that he would understand and do whatever I needed him to.

Rylan sighed then moved his head, so his nose was in my hair before inhaling. His hand on my thigh tightened, and I wondered if he could tell that I was aroused just lying in bed with him.

"Mmm," he hummed in my ear. "Morning."

"Morning." I stretched my legs.

"How'd you sleep?" He nuzzled my throat and gently kissed my skin.

"I slept well," I lied, not wanting to upset him. "You?"

"It took me a while to go to sleep," he admitted, his tone making my chest hurt.

"Hey." I turned over so I could see his face. "What happened last night wasn't your fault. You know that, right?" I searched his eyes, hoping to see acceptance, but all I saw was fear. I'd ruined the tender moment, but I didn't care. He needed to know that I didn't blame him.

He nodded his head, but I knew him well enough to know when he was lying.

"I was so helpless." Rylan growled, propping himself up on his hand so he could stare down at me. "You nearly died trying to break whatever was controlling me. You saved my life."

"Then, you saved me." I smiled, cupping his cheek. "We saved each other, which is what mates are supposed to do, right?"

"Protecting you is my job, but instead, I hurt you."

"You didn't hurt me; your aunt did. Plus, it's my job to protect you too. You're the predestined alpha that will unite the packs. You're important." I meant for my words to be reassuring, but when his lips pressed into a line, I knew that they were the opposite.

Rylan sat up, avoiding my eyes. Annoyance changed to anger

as he turned away from me. My wolf viewed it as some sort of rejection. How could he still blame himself? It hurt that I'd saved him just for him to have to carry the burden of failure that wasn't his to carry. Hopefully time would help him realize that.

I sat up too, swinging my legs over the mattress to the floor. My stomach growled loudly as I headed for the bathroom. I relieved myself then returned to the bedroom, ready to go raid the kitchen I remembered seeing. After that, I needed to check on Estella, the human part. She'd been unconscious when she appeared, and I prayed she hadn't been scared out of her mind when she woke up and I wasn't there.

Rylan grabbed my hand, tugging me closer to him, shaking me from my thoughts. "I'm sorry."

"You've already said that," I countered, unable to fight the urge to lean into him. "It's almost like you don't believe that I forgive you."

"I'm trying." He rubbed my back, and I sighed, enjoying the intimacy. "Just give me time."

I leaned away so I could see his face then stood on tiptoe, placing a kiss on his lips. The subject had a pin in it for now, but I was determined to make sure Rylan didn't blame himself for things out of his control.

Kissing him in this moment was a mistake. As soon as his scent filled my nose, his taste on my tongue, the urge to feel him everywhere overcame me. I deepened the kiss, dipping my tongue into his mouth and groaning when his grip on me tightened.

I wrapped my arms around his neck, pinning him against me as I pressed my front to his. Nipping his lips elicited a moan that seemed to travel from his diaphragm. It was sexy as hell and had the effect of heightening my arousal. My leg lifted, curling over his hip, allowing him access to the place that I desperately wanted him. Rylan grasped my thigh. His fingers moved upward to my ass cheek, pulling my pelvis into his.

I sighed between kisses, moaning as his erection rubbed me at just the right angle. My body heated as the foreplay ramped up to new levels. There was an ache inside me, a need that only he could satisfy.

A knock on the door startled us both. Rylan took a step back, his jaw clenched like he was struggling to control himself. I grinned inwardly because this was what I wanted, what I craved. The urge to complete the mate bond was an incessant buzzing just under my skin. Ready at a moment's notice.

"Uh... I've got some food cooking and coffee ready," Deacon called through the door after clearing his throat. "Oh, and your friend is awake."

I gasped, having completely forgotten that I wanted to check on Estella. Rylan was my own personal distraction, one that was proving to be a problem.

Rylan adjusted himself. I waited a beat before opening the door. Deacon was gone, seeming to have sprinted back down the hallway when he realized that he'd interrupted something.

I opened the door, intending to follow him to the kitchen, but I paused to glance over my shoulder.

"It's all right. I'll be behind you." Rylan waved for me to go.

I nodded, feeling slightly guilty for not finishing what we had started.

The cabin looked different in the daylight. My first glance had shown the walls were made of logs giving the place a rustic feel while the décor was more modern. It felt luxurious without being obnoxious. It reminded me of what my home

37

had once been. Surrounded by forest, as if it was made to look like nature itself had built it.

"Good morning," I announced, hurrying into the kitchen and finding Estella sitting at the small dining room table, her hands wrapped around a mug.

I sat down beside her, wanting to grab her hand and ask if she was all right, but I didn't want to bombard her. She'd been completely isolated in the Between, so touching might be too much for her to handle.

She looked startled when I sat down, but she quickly recovered, all trepidation falling from her face. I smiled at her, happy to see that she was adjusting quicker than I originally thought she would, her white wolf was under the table at her feet. The wolf was leaning its head against Estella's calve, maintaining contact like wolves did in the wild. I was so happy to see them together that my chest tightened as unbidden emotions rose to the surface.

"Good morning," Estella replied, her voice quiet like she wasn't used to using it and didn't know how to control the volume.

"I'm sorry I didn't check on you sooner." I hoped she wasn't upset with me.

"I was sleeping until a bit ago." She frowned, looking down at the cup in her hands. "I haven't felt hungry or thirsty in a long time. It was jarring. Thank the Moon Spirit that my wolf was there to ease my mind."

I smiled at the wolf under the table, glad that I was able to reunite the two of them, even though it wasn't in the way I was expecting. I was disappointed that they wouldn't be whole again. If I was in her situation, I'd want to have my wolf with me however I could.

38

'Agreed.'

A door on the opposite side of the table opened, and Deacon stepped through, carrying a platter that was piled high with what appeared to be every bit of meat he could scrounge up. It smelled delicious, and my mouth started to water, but I couldn't help raising my eyebrows at him.

"I'm useless in the kitchen, but I can grill," he said in response to my silent question.

"Deacon and kitchens do not mix," Rylan teased, entering and heading straight for the coffee pot. "Are you sure the coffee isn't burnt?"

"Estella doesn't think so," Deacon shot back, grabbing some plates and utensils.

"It tastes heavenly," Estella praised, closing her eyes as she took a sip.

My smile grew when she sighed contentedly as Deacon settled into the chair beside her, his eyes observing her with an intensity that I recognized.

Rylan distracted me by placing a steaming cup down in front of me then sitting in the seat next to me.

"Are there eggs? I can make some," Rylan offered, eyeing the platter of grilled meat.

"I asked Estella what she wanted to eat, and she said meat." Deacon shrugged like it was a completely normal request.

"I see." I grabbed a plate and fork then speared some sausages and bacon. As wolves, one could never go wrong serving meat.

"It smells divine," Estella said hungrily.

"It's been a long time since you've eaten, so take whatever you want," I encouraged, handing her a plate and fork.

"What do you mean by that?" Deacon's voice dropped a couple octaves.

"Mean about what?" I asked him, confused by his question.

"You said she hadn't eaten in a long time," Rylan said, watching his friend, who was tense.

"Well, she's been in the Between for decades," I reminded them.

"Start at the beginning," Rylan suggested, looking from me to the human Estella and back again.

"Something terrible happened to Estella that split her human and wolf halves apart." It was the easiest way to explain it, though I didn't have all the details on how or why it had happened just the vague answers the Moon Spirit had told me.

"Spirits." Deacon cursed, looking a little queasy. The thought of being separate from my wolf was enough to make me feel icky too.

"I was a sacrifice." Estella spoke softly as she stared at her plate that was piled high with food. "That's why the Moon Spirit kept me in the Between and promised that my wolf and I would be reunited one day."

"I can't even imagine how painful that was." Rylan sympathized.

"Being in the Between was easy. It was the separation that nearly killed us both." The wolf Estella rose to a sitting position and rested her head in the human Estella's lap, giving her comfort the only way she could.

Human Estella ran her hand over her wolf's head, scratching her behind the ears absently as she seemed to relive something terrible from her past.

"You're here now," I reminded her, placing my hand on her shoulder.

"I know. I was kept alive for a purpose, and I intend to do

40

whatever I have to help you defeat my sister."

"Wait, sister?"

"My sister is Tamra, and almost a century ago, she tried to kill me."

Chapter Seven

R ylan

Deacon and I sat there stunned. Unsurprisingly, Pearl didn't react to Estella's revelation, which meant that she knew or suspected something like this.

"You knew about this?" I asked incredulously.

"Sort of. She didn't belong in that place, and I knew she'd be able to help us. I'm not sure how. Gut feeling I guess."

My brain seemed to be short circuiting because I was having a hard time grasping the news. Estella was my aunt's sister. How come I didn't know that she had a sister?

"We're related, then," I whispered, having mixed feelings about it.

"I suppose I'm your aunt too," she replied sheepishly.

Estella looked the same age as everyone else sitting at the table. If her and Pearl's story was true, that meant that she had been in limbo for a century or more judging by how old my aunt looked. Never aging. Staying the way, she'd been when her and her wolf had been ripped apart.

"I never knew." I wondered what Ledger would think of this.

"That's why I needed your help to get her back." Pearl placed her hand on my arm. It was a comforting gesture. "You're her family."

"I needed a family member that's an alpha to call me back. I waited so long." Estella looked at me with tears in her eyes.

"It also helped that you are *the* alpha," Pearl added.

"I'm honored to have helped you return," I said, meaning every word. "Excuse me for a moment."

I pushed my chair back and rushed out of the kitchen, down the hallway to the room Pearl and I slept in. My mind reeled over the fact that I had another family besides my uncle's. Unbidden, my thoughts turned to the past and how different my life would have been if there was someone else to take me in.

Everything that I thought I knew about my past was now in question. The power my aunt had wielded at the Gala was unheard of, but it also made so many things make sense. My wolf encouraged this train of thought, even revealing that some of my actions were made against my will.

I would never betray Pearl and her family, but I was forced to. My aunt had manipulated my memories and my actions. I hadn't wanted to leave the pack and travel around, learning to be a beta, but there was an unconscious urge that forced me to go.

Sitting on the bed, I grabbed my head, squeezing my skull and trying to figure out how much of my life had been my aunt's manipulation. It made me question everything. My feelings and confidence took a hit.

"Hey, man."

I turned toward the door and found Deacon leaning against the frame and watching me with a concerned look on his face. "Hey."

"Freaking out a little bit or a lot?" he asked like he knew what I was feeling and thinking.

He'd always been that way though. He had a way of understanding emotions and empathizing with them. It was a great skill to have, and I knew he'd make a great alpha one day.

"A lot."

How could I not? Everything from last night and now, the revelation that I had family all along, was too much. Not to mention everything concerning Pearl, who was obviously feeling urges from our incomplete bond. If I let myself dwell on it, urgency would take over my mind, but I couldn't let it. Now was the time to be levelheaded, and thinking of completing the mate bond was a distraction I couldn't allow.

"Have you heard anything through your pack bond?" Deacon asked randomly.

It took me a moment to think about it and then feel around in my head before I could answer him. "No, and I don't feel it anymore either."

"It's the same for me," he replied thoughtfully. "I have a theory though."

Of course, he did.

"What's that?" I was thankful for the distracting topic.

"When you did your alpha power move last night, I think it severed our connections to our packs."

Alarmed, I stood up and started pacing the room. Wolves couldn't survive separated from the pack. We had a pack mentality just like wolves in the wild did. We needed touch and a place to belong. If one was separated for too long, the wolf would eventually turn feral.

"Shit, shit, shit." Was Pearl alright? Was she feeling the effects yet? Was I?

"Calm down," Deacon said, and like he'd flipped a switch, my mind settled. I sat on the bed again.

"Are you feeling the effects?"

"No, which brings me to my next theory. I think your power severed our connection to our packs and then reformed with each other."

"Are you saying that I inadvertently created my own pack?" I was stunned. That sort of power was rare. So rare, in fact, that only one shifter in our history had ever accomplished it.

"Yes, that's exactly what I'm saying."

"How?"

"I don't know, but maybe it has something to do with being *the* alpha your mate spoke of." Nothing got past Deacon. He impressed me.

"You figured it all out, huh?"

"No, they're just theories that may or may not be true." He smirked like he knew he was riling me up and enjoying it.

"It makes sense actually," I mused, thinking of the heightened urges to complete the mate bond, along with Deacon's intuition that seems extra touchy lately. "Can you feel me?"

"Sort of." Deacon's brows bunched together as if thinking about it.

"I can sense you when you feel something big. That's why I interrupted you this morning."

I thought back to what I was feeling with Pearl earlier. I was overcome by her, but there was also a part of me that was panicking. Pushing her away wasn't an option, neither was completing the mate bond at that moment. There was so much that I had to focus on that mating should be the furthest thought from my mind. It was aggressively at the forefront, though.

45

"It only gets worse the more you deny yourself and her."
Wise words from an unmated male wolf.

Why was I the chosen alpha again? It made much more sense
for Deacon to be the alpha to unite everyone. He was patient,
kind, and understanding to the point of being infuriating.

*'Don't question the Moon Spirit's decision. She chose you for a
reason.'*

If Deacon was the chosen alpha, he'd be Pearl's mate, and
that thought made me unreasonably angry. Pearl was mine. I
just had to figure out how to be what she and everyone else
needed. Easier said than done.

"I have to come clean about something," Deacon began—the
worst start to a sentence ever. "I invited some people over."

"What the hell?" I shot to my feet, fists clenched at the
thought of people knowing where Pearl and I were. We barely
escaped with our lives. At the very least, the packs would want
to know how a meteor had crashed the party, literally. Telling
them it was a distraction wouldn't go over well.

"It's people that I trust," Deacon said stupidly. "I was discreet
with my questions."

I growled, the sound full of menace. I trusted him with my
life, but not Pearl's. I was the only one who was allowed to
protect her, to touch her, to breathe the same air that she did.

"What's wrong?" Pearl asked, striding into the room, looking
ready for a fight.

"He invited people," I snarled, pointing at who I thought was
my friend.

"Here?"

"Where else?" I regretted my harsh tone instantly but also
felt it was justified.

"Why? I don't understand?" Pearl glanced from me to

Deacon, her posture and tone demanding an answer.

'Fucking mine,' my wolf said possessively, watching at our mate with obvious heart eyes.

'Ours,' I corrected him. He couldn't leave me out of it.

"We escaped the archives to regroup, right?" Deacon's eyes were begging me to be reasonable. "This is regrouping."

"We don't know these people. What if they're under Tamra's control? You just revealed our location." I. Was. Furious. Seriously, what the fuck?

"Before we jump to conclusions, can you give us more information on these people?" Pearl asked, her calmness annoying me almost as much as I wanted to strip her naked and throw her on the bed.

"You are familiar with them," Deacon started super vaguely, and I had to bite back a pissed off growl.

"Familiar how?" Pearl sounded a little annoyed now too with his answers.

"I know I'm being vague. I'm just not sure how you will react." Deacon didn't look at me, the growly shifter, but at Pearl.

Her demeanor changed. She went from annoyed to apprehensive really quickly, which made my wolf perk up more than he already was. I grew still, ready to act as an alpha or as her mate, whatever the situation called for.

"I know in Daywa, enforcers were found out and killed or shunned, but that didn't happen in the other packs."

Chapter Eight

Pearl

I could feel Rylan's eyes on me, watching every micromovement I made, ready to step in. I appreciated his hesitance, but in a way, I also wished that he'd get all growly. A demented part of me wanted to watch him completely lose his shit over me. It wasn't the ideal situation though. I just learned that my family's legacy hadn't completely disappeared. My father had been an enforcer, the position one that he was intensely proud of until it all came crumbling down.

It was exciting to know there were more enforcers out there but also terrible. The enforcers represented a path that I would never be able to walk thanks to Rylan's uncle. They were what I could never be, and it was a relief. I didn't have to spy for the current alpha. I'd never be shackled to the pack like my father had been.

On the other hand, how would I react to seeing enforcers? My first instinct was to walk away, let the pieces fall where they may but I couldn't. I was the Alpha Seeker. I wouldn't turn my back on them because I was apprehensive about their group because of my past. I should be viewing this as a blessing instead of something that could go horribly wrong. I had to trust that the Moon Spirit knew what it was doing, that there was a bigger power at play here.

"I suppose they are the best option," I mumbled, registering that Rylan's shoulders eased at my reaction.

"Can you give us a second?" Rylan asked Deacon, but it felt more like a command.

Deacon bowed his head and left the room, shutting the door behind him, leaving Rylan and me alone. As soon as the door clicked, Rylan opened his arms in invitation, and I didn't hesitate. I ran to him, his strong muscles holding me securely against him. Being held like this, so close to the only person who knew my pain, helped me.

"Thank you," I whispered, pressing my face into his chest and breathing in his scent through his t-shirt.

"I'm here. Always." Rylan's lips moved the strands of hair they were pressed against.

"I'll be all right with you by my side," I said, believing every word. I could handle anything that this life threw my way as long as my mate was with me.

"I had no idea he was going to do that." Rylan rubbed my back, and I closed my eyes. His attention and touch were the balm that I needed.

"I know you didn't." I hoped he knew that I would never blame him again. "It'll be all right. Did he say when they would be here?"

"No, he didn't," Rylan answered, a bit growly like his earlier temper.

I understood his frustration, and while I would have liked to have been given the option of whether or not I wanted to meet with them, I understood that people did what they thought was right, most of the time. There was a plan for every eventuality, but freewill was still a factor. Rylan trusted Deacon, which meant I did as well, and I was certain he wouldn't intentionally put anyone in harm's way.

"I'll ask him when they are expected to arrive. Take a minute, okay?"

I nodded, appreciating him more in that moment. "Okay."

I leaned my head back to accept his kiss. It was short but full of unspoken emotions.

He left the room, leaving the door ajar, giving me as much privacy as he could while still keeping an eye on me. In any other situation, it might have been stifling, but it was pleasant. I'd been alone for so long that having someone think about my wellbeing was heartwarming.

"*What?*" I heard Rylan roar from down the hall.

I was out the door and running down the hallway to the common area before I fully registered that I had moved. Rylan was furious, dark fur rippling down his exposed arms. His eyes had become greener, meaning his wolf was close to the surface, while his face had started to contort. He was on the edge of shifting, and who knew what his wolf would do if he didn't regain control.

Without thinking, I approached him, his wolf growling at the sudden movement. Deacon reached for my arm to stop me, but I avoided him, beelining for my mate, who was having trouble staying in control.

I touched his arm hesitantly, watching as his wolf eyes focused on me. The rippling of fur stopped, but his bright eyes remained.

"What happened?" I directed the question at Rylan, but from the set of his jaw, I knew he was too worked up to respond.

"They'll be here any minute," Estella answered, hugging

herself while her wolf brushed against her legs, clearly trying to calm her agitation.

"Next time ask permission instead of forgiveness or give me a fucking heads up. Longer than a few minutes," Rylan snarled at Deacon, who dropped his gaze unable to maintain eye contact.

Deacon was dominant, an alpha-apparent himself, but submission showed how powerful Rylan's wolf was. He would only get stronger from here. I needed to watch him to make sure that he and his wolf could handle the power that came with being the Alpha Seeker's mate. It worried me that the power may corrupt him, but I was determined not to let that happen.

"Yes, Alpha." Deacon spoke softly, showing with his body and his words that he understood Rylan's anger. "It won't happen again."

Rylan calmed slightly, and I wondered why he didn't correct Deacon about being his alpha.

Rylan's arm wrapped around me, pulling me closer. My earlier thoughts disappeared when he ran his hands over my body. He leaned closer, rubbing his cheek against my hair. He was rubbing his scent all over me, a clear warning to any wolf nearby that I was his.

When he was done, I did the same thing, running my fingers through his hair and touching him everywhere I could without giving our audience a show. Tension bled from Rylan as I coated him in my scent. He was marking me, but I was marking him too. He was mine.

I leaned up and pressed my forehead to his, letting my touch and scent further soothe the volatile beast inside him. His hands gripped me through my clothes, and I grew dizzy with desire. Rylan's chest rumbled under my hands as he registered the sudden spike of desire.

Leaning down, he kissed my cheek so close to my mouth that I'm surprised he didn't catch my lips. "Later," he whispered, voice strained as he fought whatever he was feeling.

I nodded, falling back onto my heels staying beside him, knowing that touch was the key to calming him.

"They're close." Deacon moved toward the front door.

Rylan nodded and faced the door, putting himself between me and the possible threat. I didn't fight it. Now was not the time to argue about the fact that I could take care of myself. His instincts were screaming at him to protect me at all costs. I wouldn't interfere with that.

We stood silently waiting. Deacon kept shooting nervous looks at Estella, who looked pale. If the situation wasn't so hostile, I would go to her. I felt an overwhelming urge to protect her. I wouldn't stifle her though; she'd been away for a long time and was still trying to regain her sea legs. The best I could do was keep an eye on her.

The wolf Estella's ears rotated, like she was tracking movement that none of us could. Senses in wolf form were ten times what they were in our human forms. Our senses were higher than humans, but wolves were on another level.

Soft footsteps approached the cabin, and I stiffened, grabbing onto Rylan's arm and hugging it to my chest. He didn't protest, his focus solely on the front door. I held on tight to help calm both of us, but also to hold him back if he decided he didn't like any more wolves in his space.

The footsteps sounded on the front porch; the tension so thick I could almost feel it pressing down on my shoulders. I took a breath, then let it out slowly as Rylan's body coiled, ready to react to whatever was on the other side of the door.

Estella whimpered, drawing everyone's attention. Her wolf was pressed against her leg, like she was the only thing keeping her human half standing. Deacon's jaw clenched at her obvious fear, which seemed to make his wolf antsy. I could see the battle he was fighting on his face. He was acting as beta, protecting his alpha, but it was clear that wasn't where he wanted to be.

Deacon took a step back toward Estella when someone knocked. Once again, we all focused on the door, barely daring to breathe as Deacon grasped the handle.

With a twist, the door was pulled open. A group of shifters of various ages and body types. My eyes zeroed in on a swatch of bright hair that stood out like blood on snow. The color was familiar, but then the group shifted, and I lost sight of it.

"Thanks for coming." Deacon stepped to the side, revealing Rylan and me.

"Alpha," the man at the front said, dropping his gaze so he wasn't looking directly at Rylan. "We're here to help."

"Pearl?" a feminine voice asked, breaking the tension.

I peeked farther around Rylan and watched as a short wolf appeared from behind the leader. Her hair was dyed bubble gum pink while the ends were a bright purple. I recognized her immediately, and if Rylan wasn't blocking my way, I'd run to her.

"Arden."

Chapter Nine

Rylan

Pearl slipped past me faster than I could react. She ran to her friend, who had tears streaming down her cheeks, eyes full of relief to see her whole.

"I thought you died," Arden wailed, wrapping her arms around my mate.

"It's okay. I'm alright," Pearl assured her, hugging her back.

I was stepping in front of the two girls before I could blink, my chest rumbling with a warning to these new wolves. Every one of them took a step back, eyes downcast as I stood protectively between them and the two friends.

I knew how important Arden was to Pearl. I wouldn't get in the way of their reunion, but I would protect them both. My wolf viewed Arden as a pack member, so we would defend her just as fiercely as we would our mate.

"How are you here?" Pearl asked the question I was dying to know as well.

"You know better than anyone that enforcers must keep their identities secret." Arden wiped tears off her cheeks.

"So… you're an enforcer?" Pearl's voice took on a steelier tone.

"I couldn't tell you before."

"I know. I know." Pearl's reply hurt my heart.

This must have been hard for her, facing the very people that her and her family used to be part of. I knew she felt like she'd been abandoned by the others, but Arden was right, she couldn't tell anyone. Enforcer secrecy kept them alive. I have no doubt that any alpha that found out who the enforcers were in his pack wouldn't hesitate to strip them of their duty.

Deacon stepped to my side, looking over the gathered wolves on the front porch. At first glance, there seemed to be about twenty in total, give or take a couple.

"What is the aftermath?" Deacon asked the leader, his eyes narrowed and focused.

My attention turned to the leader too, curious about how the packs reacted to Tamra's control and the meteor that the Moon Spirit smashed into the archives.

"Chaos." The wolf ran a hand through his curly reddish hair.

"How so?" I asked, shifting to the side so I could keep Pearl and Arden in my sight along with the gathered wolves.

"That's something that we need to discuss…" The leader trailed off and glanced around like he expected to be overheard.

"Come inside," I invited, grabbing Pearl and Arden and pulling them out of the way to allow the wolves to enter.

Deacon withdrew to the kitchen, and I wondered what he was doing when I realized that both Estella's had disappeared. I frowned, wondering if I should go see if she was all right but also knowing that four was a crowd. She was probably just overwhelmed by the sudden arrival of so many people. I empathized with that and made a mental note to watch out for it in the future.

"My name's Teo, and I'm from the Sanda Pack," the red-haired leader introduced himself.

"I'm Rylan, beta for the Daywa pack." It was an automatic response, but I knew that I wasn't just a beta anymore. Teo seemed to know it too since he smirked but didn't say anything.

"Nice to meet you." His eyes flicked to Pearl, who stood by my side.

"I'm Pearl." My mate offered her hand. My wolf huffed, annoyed by the invitation, but I ignored it. Pearl could shake hands with whomever she wished, but if the touch wasn't so innocent, I would have an issue. "Please make yourselves comfortable."

Teo nodded then turned to the living space, where the other wolves had settled on the sofa, the armchairs, or on the floor. I could feel eyes on me, and it made my skin twitch. They were curious—I could smell that in the air—but there was also uncertainty along with irritation.

"Please explain," I said, focused on Teo, who still wouldn't look me in the eye.

"You did something that freed us from Tamra's control," Arden began, strolling to stand by Teo's side and staring at me.

"It wasn't my intention, but yes, I did," I confirmed, thankful that Pearl was beside me holding my hand.

"Well, it didn't just free us from her control but from our alpha's as well."

"Excuse me?" I barked, ignoring the other wolf's flinch at my tone. I wanted to glance at Deacon and demand he explain how the hell his theory was completely accurate.

"You freed everyone." Teo glanced down at his booted feet.

"From Tamra's control and from the alpha pack bond?" Pearl asked, as if double checking that what he'd said was correct.

"That's right." Arden nodded as she watched her words sink into the both of us. "The meteor hit after that, so it's been chaotic ever since. Nice touch with that by the way. Would never have expected that."

"Every alpha is re-bonding with their pack while others have viewed this as freedom and joined Tamra." Teo interrupted, solemnly.

I wondered if I should voice Deacon's theory since it was the most plausible one we had.

"We've noticed changes too," Deacon supplied stepping back into the room, having heard my hesitation and following my lead.

"Are the wolves feeling an effect from the lack of a pack bond?" I wondered. Seeing as we hadn't felt anything thus far, maybe I'd spared others from it too.

"Yes, some more than others." Arden glanced at Teo before turning her gaze back to me. "We're all feeling the effects, but instead of rejoining our packs, we decided to come here. To the true alpha."

I was stunned but appreciated her honesty. How should I handle this? My wolf and I felt the urge to accept these wolves and add them to our pack, but was it really that easy? I didn't know them. How could I trust them? How could they trust me?

Pearl shifted her weight, drawing my attention. I was hyper aware of her in this room with unknown shifters. It made my skin itch. The different scents and emotions in the air were overwhelming. My wolf helped me filter everything, but it was still irritating.

How do you gain trust and respect from pack less wolves? I could think of only one way, but Deacon was correct. We needed to regroup and add to our numbers. If these enforcers joined my pack, it meant I could protect them from my aunt and hopefully figure out a way to free all the others.

This was the start of something big. I knew in my heart that this was the right direction, and with Pearl here with me, I was confident I could handle whatever was thrown at me.

'Are we strong enough?' my wolf asked gently.

'We'll have to be,' I countered, not looking forward to what I had to do next.

'What about Pearl?'

'Deacon will keep her safe.'

'That's not what I meant.'

I knew what he meant. The mate bond with Pearl was a distraction that we couldn't afford to have. The best thing to do would be to complete the mating then have access to all our power, but that didn't seem like the best solution. I didn't want our mating to happen just because I wanted all of my alpha abilities. It was selfish, but I couldn't deny it was intriguing. When fully mated, what would I be capable of?

"I appreciate you all coming here. I'd be happy for you to join my pack, but these are desperate times. I won't allow a wolf to join unless he or she has my respect and trust. I'm sure you feel the same way." I addressed the room, my wolf speaking the words alongside me. We were a team. "I can't promise that I can protect you from my aunt's ability, but I will do everything in my power to prevent it from happening again."

Pearl slipped her fingers through mine, silently giving me her support, which made my heart lighten.

"There's still so much we don't know about this new enemy. If you have information that might help us, please come talk to me," Deacon announced, stepping into the role he was born to play.

I couldn't help the negative thoughts filtering through my mind, but I would do my best to ignore them. This task was given to me by the Moon Spirit, and I was committed to seeing it through.

"There's coffee in the kitchen, so help yourself. I'll be outside ready to accept any challenges," I said, feeling Pearl's surprise at my words. "I want to gain your respect and loyalty. This is the best way to do it. Once you are satisfied with me as your alpha you may join my pack."

"Are you serious?" Pearl hissed, pulling me away from the room full of shifters. "You can't do this."

"I am serious. I *can* and *will* do this." I tugged her to me, wrapping my arms around her and holding her tight. "It seems to me that you don't think I can handle challenges."

She scoffed; her lips pressed together in a thin line across her face. She was worried, I could tell. It made me happy that she was concerned.

"I don't like this," she said softly, looking up at me through her eyelashes.

"I'll be fine," I assured her, trying and failing to hide my teasing smile.

"Why are you smiling? This is serious, Rylan."

"I know this is serious. I'm the one who offered to accept challenges. In order for them to look at me as their alpha, they have to test me."

"But what if you get hurt?" Her lip trembled, and I realized she was scared.

"Getting hurt is part of the process, but thankfully, I'm a shifter and I heal fast. You don't need to watch."

"I think I have to." Pearl bit her bottom lip. "You are doing this to prove that you're a worthy alpha. I need to watch so they see that I support you as your mate."

"Spoken like a true alpha female," I praised, leaning down and pressing a kiss to her lips, enjoying her soft inhale of surprise. "I'd be honored to fight for you."

"Not just for me. Fight for us."

Chapter Ten

Pearl

I was nervous. The idea of Rylan accepting challenges to gain loyalty and respect was admirable, but it made my chest clench.

"Have you ever seen him fight?" Arden asked, walking with me outside behind the cabin, where there was a clearing in the woods.

"Not recently," I admitted, wishing that I had so maybe it would calm my nerves.

"I'm sure you've got nothing to worry about."

I knew she was trying to make me feel better, but all it did was remind me of the years I spent hating him. I had no idea what he'd endured during that time. I assumed he continued his training to become the beta of our pack, but what did that even intel? Did he have to fight other betas? Just the thought of him in a shifter fight club situation made me and my wolf antsy.

The crowd from the house was outside now and spread out in a circle. Some were stretching while others were chatting. There was an even mix of female and male wolves. Teo was one of the biggest, but there were a few more eyeing Rylan like they'd like to break him in half.

It made me unreasonably angry.

I glared at every wolf that looked at me as I made my way toward Rylan, who stood with Deacon. His shirt was off, revealing all the delicious planes and ridges of muscle that I wanted to explore with my hands and tongue. I knew he was handsome—I even knew he was fit—but seeing him in the light of day in the middle of a forest shirtless made my heart palpitate.

Green irises flicked to me like he knew what I was thinking, and I swore my ovaries jerked to attention.

"Oh... fuck." I exhaled, needing to stop for a moment to catch my breath since he literally took it away.

"Are you all right?" Arden asked, concerned.

I'd explained what had happened the night before and how I was healed, but she was still worried. She couldn't get the sight of her best friend with a knife lodged in her neck out of her head. I understood that and would allow her to treat me with kid gloves. For now.

"Yep. Totally fine," I answered, very aware that I was being watched.

Arden gave me a disbelieving look, but I ignored her. Rylan had turned away from Deacon in order to watch me walk toward him. As I drew closer, I could clearly see the hunger in his eyes.

Rylan held his arms open for me to walk into, so I did, feeling an instant calmness. I could still feel eyes watching my every move. So, I stood on tiptoe and plastered my body against him. My lips found his, and I kissed him like I was dying. He kissed me back, moving against me hungerly, like he couldn't get enough. His hand found my ass, his fingers squeezing the muscle almost to the point of pain.

We parted, lips swollen and red from our kiss. I licked mine, savoring his taste while he watched my tongue. It was sexy, leaving me breathless with need. I'd never been so turned on in my life.

"You're mine," my wolf told him with all the confidence of a woman who'd found her mate.

"Ditto," Rylan replied, smiling then giving me a quick peck on the cheek.

I laughed at his simple answer, enjoying the encounter more than I probably should. Looking around, most wolves avert their eyes while a couple females held my gaze for a moment or two in challenge. My wolf peeked out at them, not about to play some dominance game. That was saved for the boys. These bitches needed to know what he was mine. I just showed them.

Smirking, I withdrew, stepping back to Arden's side, who eyed me like I'd just grown a second head then cut it off myself.

"What?" I snapped at her, irritated by the look she was giving me along with everyone else.

"You just… Pearl, never in the years we've been friends have you ever drawn attention to yourself."

"Oh… well, they need to know where I stand."

"I'm pretty sure everyone got the memo. Loud and clear."

"Good." I smiled, loving the exhilaration I felt at claiming him publicly.

"You've changed," my longtime friend said, a wicked smile spreading across her lips. "I like it."

I winked at her before turning my attention to Deacon, who had stepped forward, looking ready to speak.

"This is a chance to test Rylan as the alpha. The winner is decided by tap out. No unnecessary violence will be tolerated. Let's keep this clean."

Everyone gathered nodded their heads in understanding while I fidgeted with the hem of my shirt.

Rylan stepped forward into the circle, determination written clearly on his face as he waited. No one moved for at least thirty seconds, then Teo took a step forward like he was going to rush him, which set off a chain reaction.

Two wolves came at Rylan, one from each side. He sidestepped the first, letting his momentum carry him away while simultaneously blocking the second wolf's jab. Quicker than I'd ever seen him move, Rylan spun, kicking the second wolf in the back of his knees and making him buckle. By this time, the first wolf had recovered and rushed back, presumably intending to tackle with brute force.

Rylan jumped over him, landing behind him and punching him square in the jaw when he whipped around. The wolf fell to the ground dazed while the second recovered.

Another male with long brown hair and a mean expression ran forward, jumping over the downed wolves. His hands had shifted partway, so he could use his deadly claws. Rylan blocked the first punch then the second while backing up to give himself more space. Catching the next jab, he grabbed the man's wrist and twisted under it, forcing the shifter's hand behind his back. The wolf snarled when Rylan applied pressure. I could only imagine the pain traveling up his arm.

The fighting only got worse after that. A female snuck behind Rylan while he was engaged with two wolves and slashed his back with her shifted claws. I growled, angrily letting Arden hold me back before I charged into the mele and ruined everything. With an angry snarl, Rylan grabbed the woman by the throat and hurled her into a group of charging men, knocking them all to the ground. I smiled satisfied and proud of his actions while also wishing it had been me with my hand around her throat.

Standing on the sidelines, Teo watched Rylan face off with wolf after wolf before he whistled a sharp note. Everyone stepped back, like the order had come from an alpha.

Rylan turned, ready to face whatever the leader was planning to throw at him. Teo paced in front of Rylan, who was tense, coiled, as he waited for the man to make the first move.

Suddenly, Teo began to shift. Fur erupted all over as his body grew and contorted. At first, I thought he was simply shifting into his wolf form, but after a moment I realized he wasn't. His legs grew then snapped as the joints changed to those of a wolf. I watched in horrified fascination as he became a beast-man—partially shifted while remaining on his hind legs.

Teo reared his head back and roared, a guttural sound that made a chill run across my shoulders. A beast-man form was extremely difficult to do. The fact that Teo could manage it meant that he had alpha potential.

It was awesome and terrifying to witness. The control he had to have over his wolf would have been as strong as iron.

Rylan eyed him like he was reluctantly impressed.

"Did you know he could do that?" I asked Arden, nervous that Rylan wouldn't be able to match his opponent.

"Yes. His control is unmatched." Arden watched intently as Teo finished.

All eyes turned to Rylan, who just stood there. He shot a glance at me before he visibly relaxed. Taking a single step backward before closing his eyes, coming as still as a statue.

Everyone seemed to collectively hold their breath, waiting to see if Rylan could match the power and control that Teo had just displayed. My heart pounded in my chest ready for my mate to make his move. I wanted to reach out to him and lend him our strength, but I knew he'd never accept it. This was a battle he and his wolf needed to face alone.

My eyes were fixed on Rylan's shoulders, so I saw the exact moment that the change began. Black-grey fur sprouted from his skin, coating him from head to toe. His face contorted into a snout while his legs grew and shifted to the correct anatomical joints. The sound of bones breaking, and cartilage popping was enough to make me grit my teeth. I couldn't look away because within a few short seconds, he had completely shifted.

Teo was a large wolf, but Rylan had him beat by over a foot. He looked exactly like his wolf, just upright like a man. Black ears jutted from his skull while his tail swished back and forth with excitement.

In moments, my mate had completely transformed from a man into a beast form. Arden sucked in a breath while I secretly smirked at all the wolves who were taken aback. Rylan was magnificent. He held this partially shifted state with an ease that even I was impressed by. He'd just proven without a shadow of a doubt that his control was steadfast, and his power was limitless.

The marks on my left arm began to tingle as Rylan straightened to his full and incredible height. He looked just as surprised by the change as everyone else. My chest swelled; pride filled me up until tears gathered in my eyes.

Rylan was *the* alpha. There was no denying it now.

Every wolf in attendance bowed their heads respectfully at the shifter who was truly the very best that had ever lived.

I was so overcome with pride and love that it didn't immediately register that my arm had stopped tingling and was now burning. When I finally did notice, it was too late.

The sharp cold bite of a knife rested against my throat, making my heart gallop like it was trying to escape my body.

Rylan's massive head turned toward me when I gasped, surprised by how the situation had shifted. His green-grey eyes darkened as he took me in, then his irises moved to the knife wielder, and a shiver of pure fear raced down my spine.

Every speck of humanity disappeared, leaving a predator behind who was more powerful than any shifter before him.

I took a shallow breath, wondering how we were going to get out of this situation without killing anyone.

Chapter Eleven

Rylan

As soon as my brain comprehended that there was a blade against Pearl's throat, I saw red. Fury like molten lava took hold of me. Darkness clouded my mind, but I welcomed it, needing all the help I could get. Flashbacks of the night before had my wolf snarling so ferociously that even I was taken aback.

'Mine!' my wolf roared in my mind and out loud.

The next second, we were behind our mate and her attacker. My partly shifted hand grabbed the back of the knife wielder's throat. My chest rumbled with unsuppressed anger as my fingers squeezed, cutting off circulation to the brain.

The attacker slumped, unconscious, and I let go while sidestepping, letting the body hit the ground. It was a female wolf who had been eyeing me ever since she arrived. My lips curled as I debated, sinking my teeth into her neck and finishing her. How dare she touch what was mine? The offense was punishable by death, and while the option intrigued me, there was a part of me that advised caution.

I almost ignored it, almost picked the body up and tore into it with teeth and claws. I'd deposit the twisted corpse to my mate, a bloody gift that said I would kill anyone who dared to touch her.

My momentary pause allowed Pearl to approach, her hand reaching out to rest on my forearm, stopping me from any further action. Her brown eyes were wide with surprise or maybe fear, I wasn't sure. The latter emotion made my heart stutter in my chest. Was she afraid of me?

As if she could read my thoughts, she shook her head, drawing closer to my partially shifted body. She needed me, and that was enough to make me forget about the wolf on the ground entirely. There was nothing in this world that could keep me away from her when she looked at me like that.

My wolf receded, letting me regain control as my body tingled and shifted back to my human form. It was a different feeling than when I normally transformed. Almost like a piece of string that had been wound too tight had finally loosened. The release of tension was almost pleasurable, but it usually left me depleted and exhausted.

Adrenaline was still pumping through me now, so when I returned to my human form, I was hyped up and ready to take on the world.

Pearl's touch distracted me from the violence my wolf was urging me to unleash. She stood beside me, watching and waiting. Once I was back to myself, she fell into me. I caught her easily, her head resting on my chest just over my heart. Her shoulders relaxed once she heard my heartbeat.

I wrapped her in my arms as tightly as I dared. This was too close to what we had already experienced. Just the thought had my body shaking with anger. I couldn't believe that this happened *again*. The need to sweep her up and run away was so strong I began to wonder why I was fighting it because she needed to be protected at all costs.

I felt like I was being stretched in two different directions. The first was the pull I felt to Pearl, my mate, my love. I had a responsibility to take care of her, to keep her safe. On the other side, I felt the need to act as an alpha, a call to be what every wolf needed. How was I going to do both? I refused to choose one over the other.

"It's all right." Pearl spoke softly, trying to ease my boiling emotions, no doubt.

"You could have been hurt," I rumbled, still angry and ready to send everyone packing.

"I know, but this revealed something that we should have thought of before."

"What's that?"

"I am your weakness," she whispered, guilt clear in her tone.

"No, you're my strength." I tilted my head back and sent a silent prayer to the Moon Spirit for guidance.

'There is no need to choose between your mate and your pack,' the Moon Spirit's voice whispered in my mind. *'They are one and the same.'*

Were they though?

'Your mate is pack. Your pack is family.'

'But I'd kill for my mate,' I countered, not seeing how they were the same.

'You'd also kill anything that threatened your family. There is no separation between the two. Your mate and pack equal your family.'

Could it really be that simple?

My wolf grunted like he was annoyed that I couldn't see the two things as one. It would be something I'd have to think about more.

My attention shifted to Deacon, who headed toward me with

a serious expression on his face. He frowned at the she-wolf still unconscious on the ground, but I saw the corner of his lip tilt upward. He looked almost pleased while I just wanted to disappear.

"Well done," he said when he was closer.

I debated snarling at him. My mate being held at knife point was not a situation to be proud of.

"You handled that really well." He praised stepping over the downed wolf.

I scoffed, biting my lip and fighting the need to put Pearl behind me. My instincts were on high alert that I wanted to protect her from everyone, regardless of if I trusted them.

"I feel... volatile," I admitted, stroking Pearl's hair with my hand, hoping that touch would calm me.

"That is to be expected. Though your mate was threatened, you showed incredible restraint," Teo chimed in, back in his human form. "Not just anyone could see past the initial rage and show mercy."

"I wasn't feeling merciful," I countered, my anger reducing to a simmer now that we were talking about it.

"It wasn't the first thing on your mind, I'm sure. I think your instincts are admirable." Teo smiled like he was proud of me. I could sense his sincerity, but I didn't feel like I deserved it. While my wolf and I hadn't completely lost our shit, we were dangerously close. The next time something happened, I wasn't sure we'd be able to stop ourselves.

The amount of power I felt coursing through me was immense, with no end in sight. I'd experienced this power before, had accessed it a couple times, but this time had been different. It was easier to reach, which made me apprehensive and leery. I didn't trust it or myself not to completely lose control. I had to figure out how to harness and focus the power, so it did what I needed it to do.

A shrill scream split the air, making everyone bristle and look around for the source.

"There!" Arden shouted, pointing behind the group to the trees.

Deacon growled as I tried to figure out what was going on. Estella the human was running toward us with several wolves snapping at her heels. Her wolf's chest was coated red, like she'd just torn into something to protect her human half.

"Rylan," Pearl said urgently, drawing my attention. "Are they entranced?"

"Yes, subdue only," I shouted, pleased to see all the enforcer wolves nod their understanding and take up defensive positions.

Estella ran straight to Deacon, who grabbed her and tucked her behind him. Her wolf was snarling furiously, her teeth bared.

"Stay back," I told Pearl, who thankfully nodded and stayed where she was.

Enforcers and entranced wolves engaged in combat all around me. Arden had shifted to her wolf form and ran toward the stampeding wolves.

A black wolf speckled with white caught my eye and held my gaze. My lip curled at the obvious challenge, pulling my own wolf to the surface. I had a sinking suspicion that I knew them, but I couldn't be sure.

Power surged through me as I stared into their eyes. There was a manic air to the wolf, which worried me. He didn't seem to have gone feral, but he clearly wasn't in control, and that alone was driving the shifter to anger. Drool dripped from his jowls, and I knew I had only moments before he attacked me, and I'd be forced to defend.

'How did we do this last time?' I asked my wolf, feeling our power bubbling just under the surface of my skin. It wasn't burning like before, which concerned me.

'We were enraged because our mate had been injured. We weren't in control of our emotions like we are now.' My wolf guided the power up from our core to our chest.

My muscles bulged, and it felt like I was going to burst apart from the power filling me up. Black fur rippled down my arms as my hands shifted, claws curled and ready to tear something apart.

'This isn't normal,' I pointed out to my wolf, feeling like I was about to combust with the energy I was trying to contain.

'Think about our mate, Arden, Deacon, and Estella. They are our pack, and they are under attack. We must protect them.'

He was right. We'd formed this pack last time our power had been unleashed. The threat was staring me down, ready to engage at any moment. I had a split second to decide if I wanted bloodshed or to try to spare the entranced wolves.

It wasn't an easy decision, but I went with the best course of action.

I inhaled deeply, filling my lungs with oxygen until it felt like they'd pop like balloons with too much air. The energy was in my chest, and I envisioned it merging with the air in my lungs.

Once it had merged to a point where I could no longer distinguish the two, my hands curled into fists, and I let out a roar.

Pouring all the energy into this one action, I prayed that it worked.

Chapter Twelve

Pearl

The roar that Rylan let out shook me to my bones. Every shifter in the vicinity dropped to the ground like the pressure from the command was too much. I remained standing by Rylan's side, his power washing over me like spring rain.

I exhaled slowly when the sound ended, feeling slightly dazed by the surge of energy that laced Rylan's roar. Arden explained his powerful roar the night before. I'd been unconscious then, so it was fascinating to witness it now.

Rylan was shaking, the amount of unrestrained force he'd just unleashed was immense. I wanted to touch him, to reassure him that everything was all right, but I didn't dare. Not when aftershocks were coursing through his body. The last thing I wanted was for him to lose his concentration.

He took a deep, steadying breath before turning to me, his hand outstretched. My hand was in his before I realized I had moved, our fingers intertwining. The contact had an instant effect on both of us. Tension bled away as we looked around at the downed shifters.

Those in wolf form had shifted back to humans. Every

single one looked dazed and confused, glancing around the unfamiliar area.

Rylan squeezed my fingers gently, my eyes met his, and I saw his wolf peeking out at me, watching me with an intensity that made my heart skip a beat. I wished our mate bond was complete so that I would know exactly what was going on behind those eyes. Lifting my hand, Rylan kissed my knuckles, making my knees go weak. It was a clear statement to everyone that no matter what came our way, I would always be first.

Butterflies erupted in my belly while I debated whether I should kiss him or tie him up and go hide in a cave somewhere. His lips twitched, and I wondered if he knew what I was thinking or just guessed. Either way, I needed a stiff drink.

"Rylan," Deacon said, breaking whatever spell we were under. "Can you feel them?"

Rylan turned to face everyone, his eyes flicking to each and every person in attendance. "Yes, I can."

Arden whistled, impressed. I mentally seconded her sentiment, in equal awe of the capability my mate possessed.

"Wait… can you feel everyone?" I looked from Arden to Teo, wondering if Rylan had added the enforcers to the pack too.

"No." Rylan's lips pulled down into a frown. "Everyone else here, except the enforcers."

But why?

It didn't make sense. The enforcers were no longer bonded to an alpha or a pack. How did Rylan break his aunt's control and initiate a bond with me, Estella, and Deacon while ignoring the other pack less wolves?

'It's a choice,' a voice whispered through my thoughts.

'What do you mean?' From where I stood, it looked like the wolves had no choice in the matter at all.

'Rylan's power frees them from Tamra's influence. The wolf then seeks out an alpha. Rylan is the closest and strongest. The wolf feels his strength and choses submit.'

Did Rylan know this?

I'd have to ask him later because now wasn't the time to question his actions. He'd done what he thought was right, and now our little pack had doubled in size in less than a minute.

A loud groan from one of the shifters drew all of our attention as he rolled over, clutching his head. I looked up at Rylan in alarm. No one else was in pain; everyone else looked relieved and a little stunned.

"That's an alpha-apparent," Deacon stated, watching the man with pity.

"What's wrong with him?" I didn't understand the significance.

"Alpha-apparents, like betas, are bonded to the pack just like an alpha. I broke that bond, and now he's feeling the effects of basically being cut off." Rylan seemed unsettled but took a determined step toward the man.

"Let me," Arden volunteered, walking toward the poor guy but stopping a safe distance away.

Alpha-apparent's were dominant wolves in line to take over a pack once the old one was pushed out. They were also volatile and prone to aggression and violence if upset, which this wolf clearly was.

"Hey, are you alright?" Arden asked him gently, so she didn't accidentally startle him.

With obvious strain, the man lifted his head to look at whomever was speaking to him, hazel eyes glazed with pain and grief.

I gasped when recognition registered. The alpha-apparent

76

on the ground in pain was Alder, from the Aibek pack. Rylan told me that he was there when Faela's body was found.

Stunned, I stared at his face while he went through a transformation. The grief slowly faded from his eyes as he gazed up into Arden's face. His mouth dropped open as he looked at my friend up and down with an all-to-familiar expression on his face.

"It's the hair. I know. You'll get used to it." She smiled, completely missing the obvious.

Alder swallowed thickly, his jaw clenching as he took in the situation, though his eyes always returned to Arden.

"Wh... what's your name?" he asked, his voice was deep and gruff.

Arden visibly shivered after hearing his question, her eyes growing wide as she observed him.

"Arden," she answered in a husky whisper.

Alder glanced around like he just realized that he was surrounded by people. His nostrils flared as he scented the air, muscles bulging when he noticed the male wolves in attendance. A silent snarl curled his lips that would quickly turn into something much different.

"Alder," Rylan said, taking a step forward.

The snarl disappeared from Alder's face as he took in Rylan standing across from him, with me by his side.

"Alpha," he greeted, the word sounding strange coming from him.

"Are you well?" Rylan asked, clearly concerned but wary.

"I... I think so." Alder slowly climbed to his feet. Everyone ignored his nakedness except for Arden, who ogled him like he was a piece of candy she'd been craving for a long time.

He was handsome, with his sandy hair that was wavy enough

to look effortlessly tousled and eyes the perfect mixture of green and brown. He was any girl's ideal man, though I preferred my dark-haired mate, with eyes that made me melt every time they looked at me.

"Good. We'll get you some clothes, then... we should talk."

Alder nodded then turned to Teo, who was handing out sweatpants and t-shirts to all the newcomers.

"This doesn't make sense," Rylan grumbled, confused. "What was the point of this attack?"

"I was just thinking the same thing." Deacon stepped closer, with Estella right behind him. "If this was an attack, it was poorly thought out."

"That doesn't sound like Tamra. She doesn't do anything without a plan first," Estella added, looking around worriedly.

"I think there's something else to this," I said, wondering what I would do if I were Tamra. "She probably needs a spy, but that won't work since you broke all the bonds. She knows you can do that..."

"So, what is she playing at?" Rylan's forehead scrunched as he tried to reason out why his aunt ordered an attack.

"A sacrifice maybe?" Or a diversion?

"Why would she send *these* wolves?" Rylan glanced around, trying to connect the dots like I was.

"I might be able to answer that," Alder announced, standing next to Deacon with his arms crossed, looking uncomfortable.

"Truly?" Estella's eyes were brighter than they were. "Tamra wouldn't trust just anyone."

"You're right." Alder rubbed the back of his neck while shooting glances at Arden, who was conversing with Teo several paces away.

"If you could complete a thought, that would be really

helpful," Deacon said sarcastically, rolling his eyes.

Alder's gaze snapped to Deacon, a sneer on his face that was clear distaste for the other wolf. I could practically feel the hostility in the air, and it was already getting old. This many dominant wolves in one place was a recipe for testosterone-fueled mayhem.

"Enough," Rylan growled, snapping the two shifters out of whatever game they were playing. "What do you know?"

"These aren't all of the shifters she sent," Alder answered, turning his gaze to Rylan then dropping it out of respect. "We were just the first wave."

"The first wave?" Deacon repeated, shooting a worried glance at Rylan, who clenched his jaw.

"Teo, get the newcomers in the house," Deacon commanded quickly before he began barking orders at the enforcers who had subdued the first attack.

"You need to go with the others," Rylan told me, glancing around with clear worry.

"The best place for me is here." I gave him a look that said I wasn't leaving his side.

He jerked his head, conceding to me, but I could tell he wasn't happy about it.

"There," Estella shouted, pointing in the direction where the first group had come from.

Shifted wolves appeared from between the trees, fangs bared, ready to attack. A dark wolf in front howled, which seemed to be some sort of signal because every wolf started running toward us.

"Guard her," Rylan barked at Deacon, who stepped closer.

"Rylan?" I called, worried for his safety while fighting the urge to ignore his command.

"Stay here, Pearl. Promise me." Rylan grabbed my arm, looking truly scared.

"Rylan, what…" I managed to get out before my mate shifted into his half beast form and growled a name that made my heart stutter.

"Ledger!"

Chapter Thirteen

Rylan

I knew yelling my cousin's name would attract his attention, and I was determined to keep it. Not only did we look similar, but we also had around the same amount of dominance and strength. I'd gained more power recently and could probably easily overcome Ledger, but he knew my weaknesses.

I sent my intentions through the pack bond, letting every wolf know to avoid Ledger and let me deal with him. Ledger wasn't above fighting dirty. He would exploit anything and everything in order to win.

Knowing what I did now, I wondered how much of that was really Ledger and how much was his mother's influence. She'd been controlling him and my uncle for decades; who knew how much she'd managed to manipulate them? It now made sense why my uncle wasn't seriously upset about his true mate dying. She'd probably buried the mate bond so deep inside his mind that he couldn't draw strength from it or even access it.

I felt sympathy for both of them, but right now, the threat was my cousin. We were family, and while I hated the thought of going against him, I had to protect my mate and pack. No one else knew how far he was willing to go.

My arms shifted first, followed by my face then the rest of my body. This form was difficult to maintain, but I needed every advantage I could get.

"Promise me," I repeated, needing Pearl to understand that she could not interfere.

"I promise," she muttered, not sounding happy about it.

The truth was, I wasn't happy about it either. I would much rather have her by my side fighting every battle that I did, but my instincts wouldn't allow it. I had to keep her safe, to protect everyone, and the only way to do that was to face the threat myself.

My wolf wondered if we should roar again. If we had more time, I would say yes, but I'd just used my power to release the first wave. I had no idea if I could use it again so soon or if it would even work on my cousin. I got the distinct feeling that this wasn't going to be an ordinary fight. I wasn't battling for trust or loyalty anymore. I couldn't hold back.

Once completely shifted, I sprinted forward, intending to meet Ledger head on. He had other plans though. He saw me coming and swerved, as if intending to avoid me in order to get to my mate. I snarled, whipping around so fast I almost lost my balance.

My longer arms shot out, claws sinking into his hind flank. He growled, flipping back, his jaw snapping at my hands. I ignored him and instead hurled him back the way he'd come.

Ledger yipped when he landed, bouncing a couple times from the force of my throw. I was amazed at how easy it was to toss a three-hundred-pound wolf over fifty yards. I knew I had new powers and abilities, but I'd never dreamed they would be anything like this.

My wolf prodded, reminding me that now wasn't the time to analyze. We were in the middle of a skirmish, so we had to keep our head on straight.

Earlier, when Pearl was threatened, I'd moved faster than I ever had. It was surprising, but again, it wasn't the time to analyze. There would probably never be a right time to really know what I was fully capable of.

Ledger had climbed back to his feet, his left hind leg tucked up against his belly, obviously injured. Nevertheless, he ran at me on three legs, determined in his movements. It made me wonder just how far my aunt was willing to push her son too. Would he beat himself bloody against an immovable force? The thought made my stomach churn and my own determination to bubble up. No matter what happened, I needed to do everything in my power to stop my cousin from hurting himself and others.

The best option was to knock him out then hope I could break whatever control his mother had on him, setting him free. Knocking out a wolf shifter wasn't an easy thing to do ordinarily. Now that I had more power, however, it might be possible.

Ledger feinted to my left, but I held my position, waiting for the exact moment to strike. Since I was in my half-beast form, it was easier to move.

My cousin adjusted and came to my other side, teeth bared and snarling. His injured leg was no longer tucked against him, which meant it had healed or he was faking. Fangs snapped at my side, but I was ready, swinging my arm and backhanding him away.

The wolf recovered quickly, eyes burning with hatred as he regrouped and came at me once more. I knocked him back, drool flying in every direction. I could hear the sounds of fighting around me, and while my wolf yelled for me to pay attention to our predicament, I couldn't help but want to join my fellow pack members.

I gave control over my wolf while I took a moment to gather strength and energy in order to attempt another roar. I had to break the hold my aunt had on these wolves and add them to my pack if they wanted to be.

Ledger's teeth sank into my forearm, jolting me from my attempt to summon my alpha power. I roared as the pain registered. The scent of blood filled the air as I tried to shake him loose, but he held on, jaw clamped stubbornly.

I used my free hand to grab my cousin's snout, intending to pry his mouth open to free my arm. He snorted then growled menacingly as my claws dug into his gums. He didn't budge, which just made me angrier. A roar filled my lungs, and I pushed every ounce of energy I could muster into the sound.

I threw my head back and let loose the bellow that I couldn't hold back any longer. The sound blasted away from me as I wrung my lungs out of every bit of air I had in them.

The area grew quiet as the attacking wolves were severed from their pack bonds and the control that my aunt had over them. They all fell down unconscious, except for my cousin, who'd released my arm and was now shaking his head like he could clear the compulsion I'd let fly.

Not today.

I sprinted toward Ledger, my claws sinking into the grass below my feet to give me leverage. When I was five feet away, I leapt into the air, my uninjured arm cocked and ready. My fist connected with the side of my cousin's head with a sound like bone hitting bone. Fiery green eyes widened in surprise

84

then rolled up as his body went limp.

I grabbed wolf's throat, ready to tear it out if he was able to shake me off my blow.

"Rylan!" Pearl screamed, dashing toward me.

I relaxed, letting my wolf side recede until I was in human form again, hand still wrapped around the neck of my cousin. Blood dripped from my arm—the wound now closed on its way to being healed.

I raised my arm, palm out in a stop motion. As badly as I wanted her to keep running and throw herself into my arms, I had to subdue the wolf in my clutches first.

'Here,' the Wolf Spirit's voice whispered in my mind as something slick and cool appeared in my other palm.

Silvery-white cuffs appeared my skin started to tingle as I quickly bound my cousin. I concentrated on Ledger, wanting to know what the cuffs would do, and was surprised to see him shift immediately back to human. I tried to reach out to his wolf, but there was a cage built around him, preventing them from shifting.

"There's a storm cellar out back we can take him to," Deacon suggested, appearing at my side, his torn shirt revealing parts of his chest with pink claw marks in their final stages of healing.

"Let me." I grabbed the chain between the cuffs and lifted my cousin, bodily. "Lead the way."

I passed Pearl on my way, making sure to brush my arm against hers. Tension immediately released from my shoulders at the simple touch. My mind cleared of all the dark murderous thoughts I'd been entertaining. I wanted to drop my cousin and wrap my mate in my arms, grateful that I was myself again, but I couldn't. Not until I'd gotten Ledger to a place away from others. I had no idea if my roar had worked on him or not. It was possible he was just unconscious from my blow and would wake up the same.

Estella fell into step beside me, her wolf keeping pace as we followed Deacon toward a small hill behind the cabin. Deacon bounded up three steps and pulled open the door built into it. Darkness filled the space and beyond while the scent of cool dampness drifted to me.

Something flashed, then a bulb flickered. After a moment, the flickering stopped, and light lit the inside. Deacon stepped through first, and I followed. The floor was dirt, as were the walls and ceiling supported with wood beams.

I deposited Ledger into the corner farthest from the door. I'd gotten the sense that the cuffs would completely immobilize him, but I wasn't about to take any chances. I lifted his arms and put the chain over a hook a foot above his head then bent it easily. If he was determined, this wouldn't hold him, but maybe with his wolf locked away and weakened, it would.

"I want him guarded every second," I ordered no one in particular but instinctively knew that Deacon would make sure it happened. He was a good beta.

I turned around, intending to leave, but came face to face with Estella. She was looking past me at Ledger, her eyes studying him with her lips pressed into a grim line.

"Are you all right?" I asked her, drawing Deacon's attention away from my bound cousin.

"He reminds me of her." She swallowed, refusing to meet my eyes.

I understood her trepidation. Ledger and I looked very similar, so she could probably see the resemblance. Tamra and I weren't blood related, but I wondered if she could see some of her sister in me too.

The thought made me angry. I wanted nothing to do with my aunt. She'd nearly killed Pearl and used my hands to do it. There was no forgiving that, and I prayed that Estella would understand and not get in my way.

Chapter Fourteen

Pearl

I was positive that Rylan was avoiding me, and I had no clue why. The two attacks had taken a lot out of everyone, which made them grumpy and tired. Even Arden, who was usually unfazed by literally anything, was subdued. Quiet. It wasn't like her at all, and I wondered if it had something to do with Alder, who seemed to follow her around while also keeping his distance.

I wanted to help, but it was frustrating because I didn't know how, so instead, I threw myself into taking care of the new wolves. I fed them, listened, and even cried with them. Being controlled took a toll on all of the shifters, leaving them raw and jumpy.

It had been three days since the attacks, and it felt like I was fighting an uphill battle. I did everything I could to distract myself, but I couldn't deny the longing I felt. I missed my mate. I knew he was doing important work, I understood that, but it irked me that he hadn't wanted me to be part of the process. I was the Alpha Seeker, after all. The one handpicked by the Moon Spirit to carry out this mission.

"Would you like to come with me to the cellar?" Estella asked, jolting me from my thoughts.

I shook my head. I appreciated the invitation, but I wanted Rylan to ask me, not Estella. I got the distinct feeling that my mate didn't want me anywhere near his cousin. Ever since we'd captured him, there had been a rift between us that had slowly widened to a gaping chasm.

My wolf pushed forward, urging me to shift with a clawing feeling like an itch I couldn't scratch. It had been days since I shifted, and my wolf was growing impatient with my refusal.

I rubbed my temples, heaving a sigh as I considered going for a run. If I told anyone they would insist on accompanying me for protection. While I appreciated everyone's concern for me, I couldn't help feeling stifled. I needed to get out of this house in order to think.

"If you're sure." Estella shot me a sympathetic smile.

She could clearly tell something was wrong. Hell, I'm sure everyone could by now. I was wrung out and snappy.

My wolf huffed, making me roll my eyes at her insistence. Going for a run wouldn't hurt anything, as long as I stayed close and didn't attract attention.

"I'll see you when you get back." I gave Estella a reluctant smile.

She nodded then turned around and swung the door to the backyard open.

I glanced around nervously, happy to see that the kitchen was empty. Casually, I made my way to the door that Estella had gone through, doing my best not to act suspicious. One good thing about Ledger being locked in the cellar was the fact that I was able to shake my Deacon shadow.

Ever since I met the wolf, he had assumed the role of beta, which meant he handled the things that Rylan couldn't. It hurt to think that I had become just a thing to be dealt with next to Rylan's cousin.

Once outside, I hurried away from the cabin. Dusk was still hanging on the horizon, casting the area in a soft glow that was quickly fading. I slowed once I entered the tree line, the scent of the forest reminding me of home, helping to ease some of the tension I felt.

When I could no longer see the cabin through the trees, I stopped, stripping out of my clothes until there was nothing between me and the fast-approaching night.

I shivered as my skin rippled, the need to shift like a siren's call that I couldn't resist. My wolf moved forward as I retreated, letting my other half assume control.

The change was swift and itchy. It got that way if I didn't shift for long periods, almost like my body was just as grumpy as my wolf.

White fur sprouted over my skin while the rest of my body broke and stretched, forcing it into an altogether new shape. My muscles twinged in irritation as I morphed into a wolf.

As soon as the change was over, my wolf shook out her fur, dispelling the annoying itchy sensation. A breeze blew through the trees, rippling through white fur and making us quiver excitedly.

Bounding forward, my wolf sprang into a run, dodging trees, logs, and stumps. Crisp air filled our lungs, encouraging us to move faster until our muscles burned from exertion.

It was... freeing. To do something that wasn't to help or soothe someone else. A bit of self-care was needed. If I couldn't have my mate to help me work off this restless energy, then this form was the next best thing.

My wolf harrumphed when I compared shifting and running

to our mate. She would rather it be him. While I agreed with her, I couldn't help but feel like there was an ax hanging over all of our heads. The other shoe was about to drop, and I intended to be prepared for it.

'I think you're right,' a depthless voice whispered in my mind. *'Things are moving much too slowly. Not to mention all of the stubborn, hardheaded wolves.'*

I chuckled, amused by the Moon Spirit's frustration at the wolves it created.

The path forward depended on what Rylan's cousin revealed, but since he was showing incredible resistance, who knew if we could rely on him for information?

'Is there a way we could speed it up?' I hoped for a quick solution so we could move on from this.

'Your mate isn't thinking like an alpha.'

I frowned at the Moon Spirit's words, wondering what Rylan had done that wasn't alpha-like. Before I could ask, a softly glowing white wolf appeared beside me, keeping pace with my wolf as we ran through the trees. The wolf huffed, and I suspected the Moon Spirit was just as agitated as me.

We ran in silence for close to twenty minutes before our gait changed to a trot then a leisurely walk. Our breathing was heavy, but the cool forest air felt good in my lungs. For the first time in a while, my mind was clear of worries and doubts. It was consumed by the present as I let go of what the future held. I'd worry about it later. Right now, all I needed was the forest and my wolf.

With my mind cleared of thoughts about the current situation, I found peace. The sound of trickling water tickled my ears, drawing me toward it. A small stream meandered through the landscape, seemingly without a predetermined path. When it reached an obstacle, it simply found the easiest way around it and kept flowing. It didn't stop to worry about the path or wondering if it was going in the right direction. The stream didn't look back to see what had already passed.

That thought struck a chord within me. I could feel the inner vibration grow in intensity as I watched and listened to the stream.

'*This is how it should be,*' the Moon Spirit spoke quietly so as not to disturb the tranquility of the moment. '*Move forward and deal with obstacles as they come while never looking back.*'

I understood what the wolf was talking about and agreed, but I just wasn't sure how to use it in the current situation.

'*It will become clearer the more you let go and let what has been and what will be go.*'

Could things really be that simple?

A twig snapped behind us, and I whirled around, claws out and teeth bared, ready to fight whatever the danger was.

A black wolf with four white socked feet walked toward me, green eyes observing me and the Moon Spirit with a question in its eyes.

'*This is where I leave you,*' the white wolf informed me and then nodded its head at the black wolf.

The wolf disappeared, leaving me and my mate alone. Rylan drew closer, concern and regret written in his eyes. I looked away; still hurt from the way he'd ignored us the past few days.

A low whine sounded from our throat as Rylan's wolf took another step. The wolf froze and cocked its head, puzzled, which made me angry. How could he not see how hurt we were? How lonely the days had been while he ignored us. How much I needed to get away from the suffocating and overwhelming feelings I felt for the pack. I shook my head,

92

determined not to explain when he could clearly see we were upset.

Rylan's wolf walked closer, his head lowered, and tail tucked, like he knew I was mad and that he was the cause. He sat down beside me with about a foot of distance between us that felt more like an eternal ocean. I wanted to fix it, but I didn't feel like I was the one who needed to.

Out of the corner of my eye, I watched as he shifted back to his human form. He was ready to talk. I shook my head then turned my gaze so I could glare at him, my ears twitching so he knew I was listening but refusing to shift just yet.

"I've upset you, and I'm sorry."

I rolled my eyes at his insincere apology. Did he think he could just say sorry, and I would forgive him? He had a lot to learn.

"I'm sure my words feel empty," Rylan continued, looking away, his attention turning toward the stream. "The last thing I want is for you to feel unwanted, but that's exactly what I've been doing. I've been so consumed with finding a way to free my cousin that I've put everything aside, especially you."

My wolf grumbled, sounding like a series of small yips and whines. It didn't mean anything, but it felt nice to respond in some way.

"I haven't been the alpha I need to be. I thought I was ready and doing the right thing, but the Moon Spirit explained that being an alpha is more than just being strong. I need to be compassionate, empathetic, and aware of every member's feeling. You've been doing that, and it's been taking a toll since I wasn't there helping you.

"I'm still trying to get the hang of being a mate and an alpha. I'm going to make mistakes, but in doing so, I plan to learn from them." He sighed, running his hand through his hair, making it unruly and entirely too appealing.

Tingles ran over my skin as the change came over me. My white fur became long luscious white hair that covered my naked breasts as it cascaded around me. The markings on my left arm tingled reassuringly.

"I appreciate everything you said," I whispered, moving onto my knees and crawling the short distance to him. I settled in his lap, and his eyes never left my face while his hands gripped my upper thighs. "I'm new to this too. I may not be an alpha like you, but I am the Alpha Seeker. I'm ready to stand at your side, ready to face whatever comes our way together."

Rylan nodded, his gaze narrowing on my lips as I spoke. I ran my tongue over my top lip, watching his eyes follow the movement. He was completely entranced by me, and I couldn't help but feel satisfied.

My hands were resting on his forearms, so I moved them upward, sliding over the smooth skin of his arms and shoulders. He shuddered underneath me when my nails gently scraped his collar bone. I leaned down and softly kissed his throat, using my hands to encourage him to tilt his head back. I wanted him to submit to me.

His chest rumbled, and for a moment, I didn't think he'd do what I was requesting. But then, his head moved, exposing his throat in submission. The urge to bite him, to taste him on my tongue, was almost too much for me to fight. I hesitated for a moment, trying to reign in the raging need before I pressed my lips to the skin above his pounding pulse.

Rylan inhaled sharply, his fingers digging into my thighs as I kissed my across his throat to the other side then up to his right ear. I could feel his hardness below me, teasing me as I

94

concentrated on his neck. My mouth began to water, and I worried I wouldn't be able to resist the desire to mark him.

I moaned against his ear, wanting to show him what he did to me. Rylan pulled my hips closer, his cock teasing my entrance as I continued to explore. I nipped at his ears, enjoying the hitch in his breathing when I swept my hands through his hair and down to his shoulders. My mouth moved up over his jaw to his lips, where I stopped, hovering over them tantalizingly close but not close enough.

We froze, our mouths millimeters apart. A challenge to see who would break first. Heat pulsed through my veins the longer we remained pressed against each other. My body was revving up into an inferno that I was on the verge of jumping into. I wanted him so badly that my inner thighs quivered in anticipation.

This was the calm before the storm. I could feel it brewing in Rylan just like the fire burning inside of me.

Were we ready?

Did we dare?

Chapter Fifteen

Rylan

I was losing control. Pearl's arousal scented the air, reminding me of when she'd gone into heat two weeks ago. I was instantly hard. Instantly primed to do whatever she would let me do, and judging by her enthusiasm, she was ready for anything.

Was this the right time? Was there ever going to be a better one?

Those two questions swirled through my thoughts as I tried to decide what the right thing. The Moon Spirit alerted me to Pearl's struggles then lectured me about how long I was taking. I understood that completing the mating would give me access to all of my alpha abilities, but I didn't want that to be the reason we did it.

'It's not,' my wolf assured me gruffly. 'She is our mate. We would die for her. We love her.'

The word *love* echoed through my mind like a gong. I did love her. I'd loved Pearl since we were kids. Even when she hated me, I loved her. I left the pack because I loved her. Everything that I'd done, past and present, was because of my love for her. She was the rock that kept me grounded when darkness threatened to tear me away from everything I knew and loved. She was the only one who could pierce that darkness and banish it for good.

Why was I questioning completing the mating? It was the most natural thing between two wolves.

In a split second, I'd made my decision and prayed that Pearl had made the same one. I closed the gap between our lips. I kissed her with everything I had, pouring every ounce of want, need, desire, and love into each movement. My tongue plundered her mouth; my teeth nipped at her soft lips. I drank in every sound she made, every panting gasp of pleasure. I breathed it in. I breathed her in.

Her nails dug into my shoulders, making my cock throb. I needed to be inside her. The urge was so strong that I was having trouble thinking straight. I wanted to roll until Pearl was beneath me then plunge into her, needing to feel her around me.

'Not here,' my wolf interrupted.

I growled at him, annoyed, but knew that he had a point. I'd have her anywhere, but she deserved better than the dirt beside a stream.

With effort, I tried to think of a place I could take her. Where no one would interrupt us.

'Here will do,' a voice I recognized as the Moon Spirit said, followed by images of a small cabin not far from here. A map appeared, giving me directions. I sent a silent thank you to the white wolf and then returned my attention to my mate.

Pearl's hips rocked against me, my cock sliding through her slick folds. I bit my lip, determined to get her to the cabin and out of the open.

"Do you trust me?" I asked, moving my hands upward so I

could grip her hips.

"Yes." She pulled back so I could see her hazy eyes and well-kissed lips.

"Good."

I stood up, easily lifting Pearl with me. I turned in the direction of the cabin and started to run. I stumbled a couple times when her lips caressed my jawline and again when her hand slipped between us to grasp me.

I growled, loving every second of the teasing while also cursing the fact that I had to run. The cabin appeared between a couple of trees; moonlight streamed through the branches, bathing the area in soft white light that almost sparkled.

I didn't slow down until I was on the small porch, barely able to turn the doorknob without crashing right through it. Glancing around, I found it to be a well-furnished hunting cabin with a bed big enough for two. A fireplace was opposite it, and a small kitchenette took up the far corner. It was cozy and absolutely perfect.

I headed straight for the bed, placing Pearl on the beautiful quilt before following. My hips nestled between her legs, her junction teasing me to the point that I had to fist the blanket to keep from thrusting into her.

"Shhh," Pearl cooed, cupping my face and looking up at me.

Her eyes were dark pools that could pierce the darkness lurking in my soul. Her silver-white hair fanned out around her head, the moonlight adding a glow that made her look like some sort of angel.

"I love you, Pearl. With every fiber of my being, with every breath I draw, and every beat of my heart. My existence begins and ends with you."

She smiled, happiness clear in her eyes as they twinkled with unshed tears.

"I love you too," she whispered, tears slipping down her cheeks. I wiped them away, knowing that I'd be wiping far more in my future but looking forward to every moment as long as she looked at me like she did now. With utter trust and adoration.

Our lips met again in a less urgent way. I wanted to show her that I loved her with my body. Words only went so far. I didn't want Pearl to have any doubts about where she belonged or how much she meant to me.

My hand slid down to her thighs. I caressed her soft skin while my tongue slipped between her lips. Gently, I pushed her legs apart, breathing in her gasp of anticipation.

I paused, debating what I should do first. I wanted to taste her again, feel her legs clamp around my head as she shuddered with an orgasm tipping her over the edge. My cock jerked like it was reminding me that it was still there, ready and verging on pain.

Before I could make a decision, Pearl's hand came between us, her fingers wrapped around my dick. She pulled, guiding me forward, and I followed without question. She slid the head through her wet folds, and I saw stars. I groaned, resting my head on the bed and trying to get a grip.

"Keep going," my mate encouraged, moving my cock up and down.

I grunted, unable to form words as she moved me to where she wanted me. Pushing forward, I gasped as I entered her, using gentle thrusts until I was all the way seated inside her. My arms trembled at the feel of her surrounding me. I wanted to pull back and plunge back in, but I needed a second.

Pearl held on to my shoulders, her breathing rapid. I froze, trying to adjust. She arched under me then squirmed, and for a second, I thought I was hurting her, until I felt her inner walls relaxing around me. Fuck me. She was adjusting too.

I fought the possessive growl that had worked its way up my throat. The last thing I wanted to do was scare her with my enthusiasm. I wanted her so badly that I was having trouble with my control. My wolf wanted to step in and complete the mating while I wanted to savor every second.

After a moment of indecision, my wolf backed off, letting me resume control. A shiver ran down my spine when I pulled back then surged forward. We both groaned loudly, the friction almost more than I could handle.

Gritting my teeth, I withdrew until I was almost out before pushing forward again. The slow movements were as torturous as waiting inside her had been. Her fingers dug into my shoulder muscles as she gasped and moaned.

Emboldened, I withdrew and thrust in slowly at first, drinking in every breath and sound that my mate made. My lips found hers as I loved her, taking my time as I moved in and out. She kissed me back between sighs. Every time she said my name, I couldn't help but pick up speed, which caused her to make more noise.

I pushed myself up, looking down at my mate, who stared at me with eyes full of desire and lust. A tingle ran along my spine as I quickened my pace, her legs clamping around my hips, encouragingly.

Pearl gasped when I hit a spot inside her, making her moan my name and beg for more. She arched her back like she couldn't get close enough. I bent down, drawing one of her puckered nipples into my mouth as I continued a steady rhythm, making sure to hit the spot that made her shake.

Her fingers dug into my ass, causing my eyes to roll to the back of my skull. This was too much and not enough all at the same time. I redoubled my efforts, needing her to orgasm, needing to see her so overtaken by pleasure that only I could give her.

Before long, she was crying out with every move I made, her muscles quivering as I brought her to the edge. I scraped my teeth over her sensitive nipple, knowing that she was right there and just needed a little more stimulation.

"Rylan. Oh, Rylan." She cried out then shuddered, the movements different from the orgasm before. Her muscles clamped around my cock, making sparks dance in my vision as pleasure rolled through her.

She pushed her hips up, meeting me thrust for thrust prolonging her climax until she was yelling, begging me not to stop.

As if I could. Whatever my mate wanted, she would get.

Chapter Sixteen

P earl

The orgasm gripped me so hard that I was having trouble letting go. Wave after wave of intense pleasure spread from where Rylan and I were connected. I felt like I was locked in a pleasure loop with no end in sight.

After what felt like hours, my body relaxed, causing tears to gather in my eyes and slip down my cheeks. I had never experienced anything like that. It had consumed me. Mind, body, and soul. I didn't know where I started, and he ended. It was intense, so incredible that I was mildly frightened by it.

Something rubbed over my cheeks, whisking away the tears. I blinked open my eyes. It was a chore just to move that much. Rylan's stormy-green eyes met mine, his eyebrows scrunched together in worry, but I could also see his satisfaction.

"Hey," he said softly, caressing my cheeks again. "Are you okay?"

"That was…" I giggled, overcome by all that I had just experienced. "It was incredible."

The corner of Rylan's lip rose as he smirked at me. The worry was gone, overshadowed by the smug look on his face. I returned his smile while I stretched out my legs, realizing we were no longer connected. I frowned, trying to remember when he pulled out and why.

"You were crying," Rylan said gently, like he'd plucked my question straight out of my head.

Wait a second.

'Rylan?' I mentally pushed the question out toward him, hoping that it worked.

Rylan shook his head, looking like a wolf who had a bug buzzing around his ears.

"Did you hear that?" I asked, trying again with renewed concentration.

"Yes and no." Rylan shook his head again in irritation. "I can feel it more than hear it."

"Oh." I frowned, disappointed.

I'd heard that completing the mating would awaken abilities in both of us. Technically though, we weren't fully mated yet since we hadn't done everything that completing the bond required. I huffed, slightly annoyed that nothing new had come of it then immediately regretted the thought. We weren't doing this for the new abilities but because we loved each other. This was a commitment that I couldn't imagine having with anyone else.

"Don't worry. It'll come in time." Rylan shot me a teasing grin before running his hand down my thigh.

I sucked in a breath as awareness of where his touch registered. Heat poured into my belly, and I gasped. A spark appeared in his eyes as the color shifted to greener than gray.

My heart skipped a beat as his wolf pushed forward, needing a front row seat. Like it was an invitation, my own wolf appeared, excited to participate as well.

"Mate."

"Mate."

Our wolves greeted each other seriously, I chuckled inwardly. Wolves did not mince words or offer pleasantries. They were straight forward and brisk, something I envied about them.

"This is not... my ideal form," Rylan's wolf began, his voice deeper than it had been a few seconds earlier. "Regardless, I'm ready to make you mine."

"Pfft, typical." My wolf huffed, surprising the hell out of me, and judging by the taken-aback look on Rylan's face, he was as well.

What the hell?' I hissed at my other half. Heat still coursed through my body, and I was hyper aware of where Rylan was and what he was touching. Now wasn't the time to pick a fight.

"Have I offended you, mate?" Rylan's wolf asked, his eyes fixated on my face, studying it like he would a rabbit he was hunting.

"Bold of you to assume I want to be yours." If I was in control of my body, I would have facepalmed my forehead.

What are you playing at?' I thought we wanted the same thing, but her reaction indicated she didn't.

Green irises narrowed on my face, and I fought not to squirm under the intensity. That stare had the power to make wolves submit, but my wolf shrugged it off like it was a fog rolling over the ground.

Rylan's lip and nose rose in a snarl, his wolf not expecting any backtalk. My own face mirrored his expression, our muscles tightening in anticipation.

'Answer me,' I growled, readying to fight for control. I didn't know what my wolf was doing, but I wasn't about to let her ruin this when we'd worked so hard to get here.

"Submit," Rylan's wolf growled.

My wolf ignored the command, which impressed me. She snarled, "No."

Faster than he could react, I moved.

Clenching my thighs to hold him in place, I arched up, using my weight to reverse our positions. My hand found his throat, claws pricking his skin as I held him down. His green eyes were an inferno of rage, but he did the correct thing and remained still. He was our prey now.

"Submit," I commanded, watching his jaw tighten as he defiantly pressed against my hand. Blood swelled where my claws punctured, filling the room with the smell that instantly made my mouth start to water.

As a wolf shifter, I'd never craved blood like my wolf did, but this was entirely different. She wasn't the only one craving it now. The difference was that it was our mate's blood that we wanted, that we hungered for, craved. The scent of it was enticing to the point where we leaned down in order to smell the trickles of blood better. A fire ignited in my core, making me gasp as need surged through my mind.

I panted, trying to get control of myself, but my wolf was lost to the lust our mate's blood had sparked. With my hand still on Rylan's throat, I reached with my other hand and grasped his erection. Rylan snarled when my fingers wrapped around him, his cock jumping in my hand.

Grinning, I guided him to where I wanted him then sat down, impaling myself with him. Taking him as deep as it would go, I watched his eyes roll when he was fully seated inside me. My breathing was shallow as I adjusted to the invasion, biting my lip to keep from moving.

"Fuck." Rylan gasped, eyes snapping open to stare up at me, desire written all over his face.

"Do you like this?" my wolf asked, squeezing our inner muscles around his shaft, eliciting a groan. "Submit and you can have it."

Irises hazy with want met mine, a challenge in their depths. *You'll break first.* I gritted my teeth and tilted my chin up, determined that he would be the first to give in.

He didn't move, but neither did I. I could read defiance in the way his jaw flexed, which just made my resolve to resist that much more difficult. My wolf debated on what to do next while I waited, so turned on. I was on the verge of begging her to stop this ridiculous game.

An idea popped into my head that my wolf immediately bounced on. Rylan's wolf was unmoving under us, and our objective was to make him submit to us. What better way than for us to seek our own pleasure?

With my hand still on his throat, I rolled my hips biting my lip, so I didn't cry out. I moved again, eyes fixated on his face, watching every emotion that flitted across it.

Stubborn wolf.

I ran my free hand up my stomach until I reached my breasts. I gave one a squeeze before running my fingers over my nipple, feeling the skin pucker. Rolling my hips again, I couldn't help a rough exhale as the feel of him inside me, plus my own teasing touches, pulled me closer to the edge.

I gasped and moaned, using his prone body as I saw fit, my hand still on his throat. My movements became jerky as I rode him, the feeling indescribable. My wolf started to whimper as we tried but couldn't get in the right position. Rylan's breathing was labored as he watched us struggle, the muscles in his jaw clenching and unclenching.

My wolf growled in my head, frustrated by the lack of

involvement on Rylan's part. The whimpering, gasping, moaning, and touching was all just a ploy. A game to get Rylan and his wolf to submit to us.

I didn't see why it was so important until my wolf explained that, as our mate, we were the only ones he should submit too. This wasn't a battle of wills like I had thought. We were proving a point. The point being that, once he submitted to us, then we would submit to him. As his mate, I came before everything else. If I was going to be vulnerable with him, he needed to be vulnerable with me first. He had to prove that we could trust him.

I felt a change in him as my wolf explained everything to me, like he was listening in to our conversation. His hands gripped my hips as he repositioned in order to push his hips up into me. My head fell back, the angle and force of him enough to make me see stars.

Through lust-glazed eyes, I watched as Rylan's whole demeanor shifted. Gone was the stubbornness, replaced by acceptance. He was submitting to me the only way he knew how. I shuddered an exhale, finally able to relax.

"Thank you," my wolf whispered with my voice.

"Anything for you," Rylan said, voice still the deep baritone of his wolf.

With his hands on my hips, he guided me as I chased my pleasure. I removed my hand from his throat and placed both on his chest, using him to leverage my body up and down, meeting him thrust for thrust.

Tingles ran from my scalp all the way to my toes as pleasure crashed over me. I cried out when Rylan increased the pace, pounding into me until he was drunk on the feeling of me.

Before my orgasm had completely wrung me out, Rylan

sat up, his arms wrapping around my back to hold me up. Somehow, he positioned himself, so he had a better angle. I gasped when he hit a spot inside me differently, making me come even harder.

Rylan's lips caressed my chest, moving upward until he reached my shoulder. He licked the skin where my neck met my collarbone, and I shivered. My nails dug into the skin of his chest, the scent of blood wafting through the air.

Rylan panted, his breath coming in quick succession as he tasted my skin while still thrusting into me. I felt like a sack of bones, so dizzy from the rush that I barely recalled that Rylan hadn't came yet. Not once.

His teeth scraped my collarbone, I moaned and leaned my head to the side so he had better access. At my submission, Rylan sank his teeth into my skin. The initial sting caused me yell, until the pain subsided. My senses were overflowing with my mate's scent; he surrounded me completely, imprinting himself inside and out.

Fangs pierced my gums as instinct took over. My jaw stretched open, my teeth sinking into the back of Rylan's neck. He shuddered but didn't pull away, didn't remove his mouth from my skin. Blood welled from the wound I inflicted, the scent tickling my nose. I pressed my lips to his skin, licked and sucked the blood that dripped out of the puncture wounds.

When the taste of him hit my tongue, I pulsed again. My inner muscles clenched so tight around his cock that I thought I might hurt him. With a muffled roar, Rylan jerked inside me, pushing up as far as he could.

On another level, I felt our souls reach for each other. Connecting. Completing the mate bond and filling me with Rylan's love. For the first time in my life, I felt whole.

Chapter Seventeen

Rylan

Pearl was limp in my arms, so overcome with the completion of the bond that she'd passed out. It wasn't unusual, so I let her adjust in her way.

I was buried so deep inside her that I never, ever wanted to leave. I could live here. The taste of her blood still coated my tongue, making me want another mouthful.

Reluctantly, I laid Pearl on the bed, pulling out of her gently, so as not to disturb her rest. I flopped down on the bed beside her and took a deep breath to calm myself.

I could feel her now in my head, like her mind had become a part of my own. She was part of me but also an extension. I could feel her in the very fiber of my being. In that moment, the only thing I could feel was gratitude. She accepted us then, bonded with us. For a moment, it felt like a dream, until Pearl rolled over, her unconscious mind reaching for me.

I held her close, going over my life up to this point, and I couldn't think of any other instance where I was completely and utterly sated. With Pearl pressed against me, her breath tickling my neck, I felt incredible. Happy. Whole.

This was where I belonged. This was where *she* belonged.

Having a mate was the biggest honor I could have in this life, and I was eternally grateful to the Moon Spirit for mine.

* * *

This place was... suspicious.

I didn't want to alarm Pearl, so I kept my thoughts to myself until she was asleep. My wolf and I scented the air, and like every other time, there was nothing amiss.

Which is suspicious.

My first clue was when I couldn't reach any members of my pack. I couldn't check in, and it made my wolf's fur stand up. The second clue was the absence of the sun or anything that could be considered daytime. It was dark, and the moon and stars lit up the sky. Constantly.

It was unnerving, but the absence of danger calmed me and my wolf until Pearl fell asleep, then we were back to worrying. Sleeping was out of the question when I knew nothing about where we were.

I reached out to the Moon Spirit several times with no answer. It had pointed us toward this location, so it should be safe. I doubted the Moon Spirit would send us somewhere that wasn't completely secure.

I kept telling myself not to worry. We trusted the Moon Spirit, but it was different with Pearl here too. If she wasn't, I might be able to relax and enjoy the solitude. With Pearl here, I felt antsy, like my wolf could crawl out of my skin at any moment.

"Awake again?" an angel's voice asked sleepily.

"Can't help it." I grinned and leaned over to kiss my mate's plump lips.

"Hmmm," she hummed, wrapping her arms around my neck as she deepened the kiss.

I sank into her, letting her distract me from my earlier thoughts and worries. The only thing I needed was my mate in my arms.

"You seem distracted," Pearl stated, breaking the kiss and gazing up at me. "Is everything all right?"

A quick reply was on the tip of my tongue, but looking into her deep russet eyes, I knew I couldn't lie. She was my mate. If she cared to dig, she could find the answer in my mind, but asking meant she wanted me to tell her. Which required admitting that I was worried about our pack and all the suspicious things about this cabin.

"I'm worried about our pack." I rolled onto my back with a heavy sigh.

"And?" Pearl prompted, knowing there was more.

"And this place is... weirding me out."

"How?" She glanced around the room quickly. Not to find anything suspicious, she returned her gaze to me with an eyebrow raised.

"Well, it feels like we've been here a few days, but nothing has changed."

"Changed?"

"Like the time of day. It's been nighttime for ages now with absolutely no change. It's like time stopped."

Pearl frowned then scooted over to the window to look outside. The moon was in the same position in the sky, as were the stars. The trees were still, and the area was quiet, like all the nocturnal animals avoided this place.

"Where are we?" Her worry seeped through the bond, making me growl inwardly. I did not want to worry her.

"I honestly don't know," I answered.

"But... you brought us here."

"Yes, but not because I knew it. The Moon Spirit gave me directions." I used my fingers to put quotations around 'gave me directions'.

"What do you mean?" The frown still on her face made my chest clench.

"The directions just sort of popped into my head, so I followed them," I replied sheepishly.

"That's good, then, right?" Her concern bled from her in a sudden rush.

"I guess. I've been trying to reach out to the Moon Spirit, but I've gotten no reply." I shrugged, unsure why I was being ignored.

"There has to be some reason." Pearl flopped back onto the bed beside me. "Maybe this is its way of giving us space?"

"By cutting us off from the pack?" It didn't seem like a good thing since I was the new alpha.

"I don't think we've been cut off," she mused, rolling onto her stomach and putting her naked ass on display. "I can still feel the bond to the others, so it hasn't been severed."

"True," I murmured, my attention homing in on my delicious mate.

"I'm sure when we're ready, everything will be restored."

I grunted, barely acknowledging her words as my hand caressed her ass. She sighed when I climbed over her and moved her long silvery hair away from her neck. I nuzzled the junction of her shoulder and neck, knowing it would immediately turn her on. That was the beauty of this place: it allowed me to learn my mate. It took time and dedication, but I was up for the challenge.

Moving backward, I grabbed Pearl's hips, tugged them up, and settled behind her. Arousal filled the air, making me and my wolf ravenous. Pearl moaned as I put her into position, and I could tell she loved the way I took charge. I ran my fingers through her slit, finding her nearly dripping and ready. I guided myself to her entrance, my jaw tightened when I became fully seated inside her. I took a moment to catch my breath, knowing from experience that it was entirely too easy for me to finish before we'd even begun.

Once I had a hold of myself, I leaned over, wrapped my arms around her, and pulled her back up to my chest, still seated deep inside her. Pearl groaned. Her left arm raised so her hand could grip the back of my neck. A tingle ran along my spine when her nails grazed the nape of my neck. She knew what that did to me.

With one hand gripping her hip and the other wrapped carefully around her neck, I leaned back then thrust up into her. She gasped, her inner muscles clenching around my invasion, making me grit my teeth.

During our first time together, when she orgasmed on my dick, I vowed to always make her come first, or twice if I could manage it.

I shoved my erection in and out, all of my attention on the sounds she made. Her gasps and sighs turned to moans then cries as I brought her closer and closer to the edge.

"Rylan," she cried out.

I pounded into her, using her body as leverage to keep thrusting so I could prolong her pleasure for as long as I could. She cried out with each additional thrust. My balls tightened, and I knew I didn't have any more time. Reaching around her, I found her clit with my fingers and rubbed the sensitive nub until she gushed, coating me with her release.

Grunting, I buried myself as deep inside her as I could go. Her muscles twitched while I emptied myself into her. Pearl rolled her head back to rest on my shoulder. I wrapped my arms around her, holding her to me for a moment so I could send a quick grateful prayer to the Moon Spirit.

Gently, I laid her down on the bed. Her eyes were closed, and her breathing was even. I collapsed beside her, out of breath and still feeling the aftereffects of my own climax. This wasn't the first time Pearl had seemed to lose consciousness, but I wasn't worried. She always recovered quickly and was ravenous for more.

Chapter Eighteen

Pearl

Waking up wrapped in Rylan was the best thing I'd ever experienced. His even breath tickled the back of my neck, making me smile. The little cabin was dark, the only light coming from the moon outside.

I didn't how long it had been since Rylan voiced his worries about this place. Days? Maybe a week? The lack of sunlight made it hard to count the passing of time. I wasn't worried though, since the Moon Spirit led him to this place.

Rylan mumbled something in his sleep then rolled over, releasing me from his hold. I remained still, listening to his breathing, wondering if he was about to wake up. A soft snore told me that he was still sleeping and probably would be for a while longer yet.

Carefully, I rolled to the edge of the bed and swung my legs over. My bare feet touched the cool floor, and I shivered, though I didn't feel the cold like a human would. I stood and made my way to the door, a need to breathe in fresh air overtaking my mind. My wolf stirred inside restlessly. The urge to shift and run was appealing, but fresh air beat it.

Pulling the door open, I stepped out onto the small porch

and filled my lungs with cool air that was surprisingly sweet. I looked around, not recognizing anything familiar about the area. It didn't smell any different than what I was used to back home.

The moon hung full and suspended in the sky. Stars splattered the blackness, barely discernible from the overshadowing moonlight. I took comfort in the normalcy of this place. I tried to find constellations in the sky. I frowned, annoyed it took me much longer to spot the Big and Little Dipper. Their locations were correct, but they were inverted.

The longer I stared, the more they started to look like reflections in a mirror. I frowned, was I just remembering them wrong?

A flash of white from the corner of my eye caught my attention. A white wolf appeared from between the trees, deep blue eyes watching me intently. I smiled, inviting the Moon Spirit to come closer.

'It's good to see you,' I greeted.

'All is well.' The wolf trotted closer before sitting and looking at me expectantly.

I lowered beside the wolf, crossing my legs and not bothering to cover my nakedness. 'What is this place?'

'This was my gift to the original Alpha Seeker and her line, but now it's yours and your mate's. This place is a small consolation for the burden I have placed upon both of you.'

'What do you mean by 'consolation'?'

'This is a getaway for you. A small pocket of reality that I created so that you might escape the burdens of reality. In this place, time pauses. No matter how long you stay here, it will feel like only minutes when you return.'

'So, it's like a reflection. A place that mirrors a small portion of *the forest that we can access whenever we want.'*

'*Essentially, yes,*' the Moon Spirit affirmed, its ears twitching as the sound of Rylan stirring reached our ears.

'*Only minutes will have passed back home?*' I was having a hard time wrapping my mind around the idea that time would just pause while we were here. It felt like we'd been here for weeks. If it was only a few minutes, then that meant that Rylan had no cause to feel guilty for being away for so long because we weren't technically gone for a long period of time.

'*Mate,*' Rylan's wolf whispered, obviously more aware than his human side.

'*I'm outside,*' I replied, amused.

'*Why?*' The inflection of the mental voice changed, meaning Rylan's human side was awake now.

'*The Moon Spirit is here.*'

'*Ah,*' was his reply, all drowsiness forgotten. *I'll be right there.'*

I could tell that Rylan had a ton of questions for the Moon Spirit. I was excited for him to learn about this place and what it could mean for us in the future. A safe space to get away. It was an incredibly thoughtful gift, one that would be enjoyed for many generations to come.

The thought of future generations made me think about what our future would look like. At the moment, the only thing we could focus on was this situation with Rylan's aunt. We needed to figure out how to rebalance the scales or there wouldn't be a future for any of us.

It was a sobering thought.

Rylan approached, sitting next to me and putting his arm around my shoulders. His face was solemn, and I knew that he'd listened to my earlier thoughts.

For the first time in what felt like weeks, we were thinking of the small pack we'd put together. Guilt ate at my insides, but I couldn't bring myself to regret the time we spent here together. Our mate bond was complete, strong, and vibrant. I would never regret that.

'I apologize for not explaining, but you both seemed... preoccupied,' the Moon Spirit said, speaking into both of our thoughts.

'So, this place is a pocket that time doesn't touch?' Rylan seemed to grasp everything we had already discussed.

'Correct.'

'Well, that's interesting.' A spark of curiosity entered his thoughts. *'I'm grateful that you let us use this place.'*

'Like I said to your mate, this place is now yours. All you have to do to find it, is follow the directions I originally gave you.'

'And... it'll work wherever we are?'

'Yes.'

"This place is incredible."

I agreed with my mate. This gift was almost too much to accept, but I didn't voice that in case I offended the Moon Spirit. Rylan slipped his hand into mine, squeezing my fingers in agreement.

'I overheard you saying that all was well?' Rylan queried, and I felt him prodding the place where the pack bond was.

'It's still there,' the Moon Spirit assured him.

'What now?' I leaned back with my free hand supporting me. *'Do we just return and pick up where we left off?'*

'Yes, but also no. You need to get information out of your cousin, but you've been going about it the wrong way. He is suffering while you're trying to get through to him. In this, he needs both of you.'

'I don't know how I can help,' I grumbled, the memory of Rylan's complete focus still caused a bit of pain.

'You are the Alpha Seeker. Your duties do not end now that you're

mated. You are still important to how the future plays out.'

The Moon Spirit's words warmed my heart. During that time, I'd felt useless, but maybe now, I could help Rylan as an equal.

"You've always been better than me." He leaned over and kissed my forehead. "I'll never be your equal."

I bit my lip to stop the absolutely cheesy grin because the Moon Spirit was still there and now was not the time to seduce my mate. Rylan's green eyes grew steelier as he caught the direction my thoughts were going in.

'How do we return? When we're ready, I mean,' I asked, doing my best to refocus my thoughts.

'The same way you got here, just in reverse.' The Moon Spirit stood up and walked several steps in the direction it had come from. *'When you are ready, and not a moment sooner.'*

With those final words, the white wolf disappeared into the tree line, leaving Rylan and I alone again. Out in the open. And naked.

He tugged me closer, capturing my lips with his as he pulled me until I was straddling his lap.

"When do you want to go back?" I eased away so I could see his face.

"When we're good and ready," was his quick reply before kissing me again.

I closed my eyes, focusing on the present. Reality would be there, waiting for us when we returned. Best to enjoy the time we had together now.

Rylan lay on the ground, his hands exploring my body as I eased myself down onto his waiting erection. My eyes closed as I settled on top of him, letting his hands run over me until I couldn't stand being stationary any longer. I braced my hands on his chest then moved my hips, forcing him deeper into me.

He groaned, his fingers digging into the skin of my hips as he watched me. There was something about being outside in the fresh air with the stars and moon shining down that was erotic. My nipples puckered in the cool air, the sensation made me gasp as pleasure shot straight to my core. I couldn't get enough of this feeling. It was one thing to feel him through the mate bond and a whole other thing to physically feel him there while inside of me. It took intimacy to another level. I loved listening to his thoughts while I was in control. The way he completely worshipped me, body and soul, was indescribable.

I arched my back as the edge drew closer and closer, my cries echoing as I struggled to keep the rhythm going.

"Keep going," Rylan encouraged, his jaw muscles twitching as he watched me.

"I can't," I protested as a shudder ran through me.

"Yes, you can," he gritted out, breathing heavily, his body like stone beneath me.

Rylan shifted slightly, his hands gripping my waist. I moaned when he helped lift me up and down, his hips thrusting me up to meet me.

"Yes, Rylan. Oh, spirits. Yes," I yelled as intense pleasure rolled through my body. My muscles tightened, gripping his cock until I thought I was hurting him.

"Fuck." He groaned, the veins and tendons in his arms popping as he struggled to be patient and wait.

Panting, I slumped, my arms barely able to hold myself up as aftershocks buzzed through me. Rylan's eyes widened as when his own climax overtook him, his hands helping to keep me upright.

When he was done, he released my torso and I fell against

him, my head resting on his chest. As we laid there in the open, with only the stars and moon as witnesses, I didn't think we'd ever be ready to go back home.

Chapter Nineteen

Rylan

I watched Pearl's chest rise and fall with her even breathing while she slept, the sheet barely covering her nakedness. Just looking at her made me want to sink into her. The lust I had for my mate wasn't something I was ashamed of, even though it seemed to occupy my mind more than anything else. I couldn't get enough of her taste, her smell, the way she sighed when I entered her, like I was the only thing she needed.

My thoughts revolved around her, but there was something tucked away in the back of my mind that I'd been ignoring. Until now. My wolf was restless, pacing back and forth in my head, urging me to think about our pack. He understood that time stood still here, but the call to duty weighed heavily on him. I couldn't ignore his insistence any longer.

As much as we both wanted to remain here wrapped up in our mate, we both knew that it just wasn't possible. There was work to do back home, and I'd be lying if I said I wasn't itching with anticipation. I wanted to get to the bottom of what my aunt had done to my cousin then figure out a way to save him and every other wolf under her thrall. It wasn't an easy straightforward task, but I was nevertheless looking forward to the challenge.

I turned away from my enticing mate, knowing that if I stared at her too long, I'd be waking her up for another round. She was exhausted, and honestly, I was too. Not that I'd ever get tired of loving her.

My skin felt tight, and the urge to shift and run for several miles was in the forefront in my thoughts, but I wouldn't leave Pearl, even though I knew it was safe here. She was the most important thing to me, and part of me wished she would stay here where it was safe, but I trusted the Moon Spirit. I needed Pearl by my side for whatever was about to come our way.

"You're thinking really loudly," my mate said, wrapping her arms around me and resting her head on my shoulder. "Is it time?"

I sighed, knowing that it was but also hating it. This bubble that we'd created was everything, and I didn't want to leave it.

"I think so." The words tasting like ash.

Pearl tightened her hold on me, and I could feel her reluctance and her agreement. It was time to get back to reality. Our pack needed us.

"We don't have anything to wear," she pointed out, making me smile ruefully.

"I remember where I left our clothes," I assured her with a chuckle.

Explaining where we had been to out pack wasn't going to be easy. The Moon Spirit said that it would seem like only minutes had passed when we got back, which meant that in a few minutes, Pearl and I had completed the mate bond and were well sated.

That couldn't happen in just a few minutes, that was for sure.

"Are you ready?" Pearl asked, her concern coming through the bond. She was worried about me and still feeling hurt that I had ignored her before.

I hadn't been ignoring her, just trying to keep her safe. I'd still protect her, but I needed her by my side more than ever. We were a team, partners, and I needed to start seeing her in that role.

"Yes and no," I admitted, bending so my head rested in my palms. I didn't want this to end but knew that it would eventually.

"I feel that." She inhaled deeply while nuzzling my shoulder.

We sat in silence for several minutes, neither of us willing to break the serenity that surrounded us. My wolf nudged me, knowing that it had to be us. I scrubbed my face with my hands before running my fingers through my hair.

No time like the present.

I patted Pearl's arms that were still wrapped around me. When her hold loosened, I stood and stretched. My muscles pulled and burned, but it felt good. Turning, I offered her my hand; she took it, and I helped her stand. Interlacing our fingers, I brought her hand up and kissed it. She tasted incredible, and the need I had for her bubbled to the surface. I tapped it down and locked it away. There would be time for more when all of this was over.

* * *

Leaving the cabin wasn't easy, and I could feel Pearl's sadness to see it go. I led her through the trees in the direction we had entered, recalling the directions the Moon Spirit had given me and following them in reverse.

I thought that we'd feel something once we left, but the transition felt like we were just walking through the forest. The smells were the same, as was the temperature. The air didn't seem different either.

When we came to the stream, I pulled my mate to me and kissed the top of her head, taking a moment to appreciate the place where we decided we were ready. I smirked, remembering her anger that was justified but also adorable.

We continued our trek and soon arrived at the place where we'd left our clothing. I'd spotted the pile when I went after Pearl and took my own clothes off and shifted so I could track her. We dressed quickly then headed in the direction of the safe house hand in hand. Neither of us spoke, choosing instead to draw comfort from our mate bond.

The pack bond was there, and I could once again access each member through it, but I refrained. Each member deserved privacy, and I would respect that unless I had reason to believe that one or more of them were in danger.

The sloping roof of the safe house came into view first, followed by the face of my second in command, Deacon. He frowned as we approached, probably sensing that something was different about us.

"You've completed the mating." It wasn't a question, more like an observation.

"We have," I confirmed, pulling Pearl to my side.

Now that we were back, I couldn't ignore the need to have her close. Touching her was both a comfort and a curse.

"Anything to report?" I knew that there wasn't but still needed to ask.

"Estella is asking to see Ledger." A muscle twitched in his jaw.

So far, it had only been Deacon and I interrogating Ledger. The Moon Spirit advised me to include Pearl. Maybe Estella could help too. If anything, she was family.

"I'd like to talk to her first." I tried not to read too much into Deacon's look of astonishment.

"Oh, all right," he murmured, turning to lead the way to the outbuilding that was my cousin's temporary prison.

I kept Pearl pressed against me; each step we took toward potential danger had my instincts screaming at me. My wolf balked at the idea of her being anywhere near a threat, but he also understood that she was our partner, chosen by the Moon Spirit. She was our other half, and we couldn't keep her in a cage, no matter how badly we wanted to.

Estella stood by the door that led to the cellar built into the hillside. Her wolf was beside her, pressed against her leg, like she was trying to transfer her strength to her human half. I had no idea if they could do that since they were separated.

"Estella," I greeted, giving her a kind smile. She returned it but it wobbled with nerves. "Deacon says you want to see Ledger?"

"Yes, I..." She trailed off, looking frustrated as she tried to find the words. "I think I can be of help."

Pearl squeezed my hand, but it wasn't necessary since I could feel her emotions like they were my own. She thought it was a good idea to include Estella. I wasn't so sure, but I trusted my mate. Plus, Estella is Tamra's sister, so her insight might prove to be invaluable.

I took a moment to reorient myself. It had been three days since the attack, not including the time Pearl and I had in the other cabin. I'd spent hours with Ledger, trying to get through to him. He never spoke, and I wondered if he even knew where he was. He didn't acknowledge my presence in the room or anyone else's. Freeing him from his mother's control was the right thing to do, but somehow, along the way, it appeared that Ledger had lost himself.

"I haven't had much success with him," I admitted, hating that I didn't know how to help him. "He's free from Tamra's influence, but with it gone, there may not be any Ledger left."

"Have you tried speaking to his wolf?" Pearl's brows furrowed with worry and concern.

"I can't seem to reach him." I shrugged.

"Interesting," Estella mused, reaching down and stroking her wolf's head behind the ears.

I glanced at Deacon, curious to see what his reaction to Estella's request was, and I wasn't surprised to see him visibly upset. We hadn't spoken about whatever this was between the two of them, but he was definitely feeling some sort of way about her. I made a note to speak to him after this, one on one.

Opening my mouth, I intended to ask how Ledger had been since I'd been gone, then I remembered that time had paused here. It had only been a few minutes, but it felt like weeks had passed.

I shook my head in an effort to get it screwed on straight.

It's something we'll both struggle with for a time.

Pearl was right. I'd need to explain everything to Deacon eventually, but now wasn't the time.

"Let's all go in," I suggested, dropping her hand and stepping toward the door.

"Are you sure that's wise?" Deacon asked carefully.

"Nothing else has worked so far. Time to mix it up." I grabbed the door's handle and pushed it open.

The space was just as I'd left it. The floor was dirt, as were

127

the walls and ceiling with wood support beams. It smelled of earth and stale body odor. Ledger was in the same position he had been in since I put him here. He sat in the corner, his wrists manacled and raised above him. His head lulled on his neck, like he didn't have the strength to keep it steady. His green eyes were open but distant. It looked like he wasn't aware of anything going on around him.

A pang of worry stabbed my chest. Did I do this to him? Was this my fault? In trying to save him, had I made whatever Tamra had done worse? Every other wolf seemed to recover perfectly except for him. There had to be more going on.

Everyone squeezed into the small space, the temperature instantly rising a few degrees. Ledger didn't acknowledge our entrance. He just continued to stare, his eyes glazed and unfocused.

"Ledger?" I asked, speaking firmly, trying to jolt him, but he didn't react.

I had no clue what else to do. I'd removed the control and freed him, but it didn't appear like he was free at all. I didn't know how to help him, and desperation returned in full force. My mind whirled as I tried to come up with something, but my thoughts were interrupted when Pearl stepped to my side. She was a soothing presence, her touch calming the sea of anxiety I was trying to navigate.

The Moon Spirit said I could help.

I had no idea how she was going to do that, but I was willing to give just about anything a shot.

Chapter Twenty

Pearl

Seeing the once-arrogant alpha-apparent slumped in the corner of the cellar, completely vacant, was disconcerting to say the least. Ledger's usually bright green eyes were now glazed over like he wasn't seeing anything. He looked lost. He didn't even acknowledge that we had entered.

"Has he been like this the whole time?" I asked, alarmed at the state of him. Something was not right here.

"Yes, he hasn't moved even a little bit." Deacon stood between Estella and Ledger, like he thought the latter would suddenly wake up and attack.

Nothing like that happened. Estella was watching her nephew with curiosity and a little horror. I couldn't imagine what she was thinking. This was her sister's child. He'd obviously been abused his whole life, made to comply with his mother's influence. There's no telling how much he suffered over the years.

Taking all of that into account, I doubted that any of us knew the real Ledger. If there was anything left of him.

My arm started to tingle with a slight burning sensation. I sucked in a quick breath, not expecting the sudden feeling.

Rylan whirled around, his steely green eyes searching for danger while I lifted my arm and stared at it. The filigree-like markings pulsed slightly with silvery-white light. I touched my wrist, expecting to feel something, but it didn't feel any different.

"What's going on?" He caressed my skin, which increased the burning sensation.

Hissing at the pain, I jerked away. The intense burning stopped when he was no longer in contact.

This is weird.

I'd always associated tingles with Rylan or people I could trust. The burning now at my mate's touch was terrifying. What did it mean? There was no way that he had done something to make me question my trust in him. So, the tingling and burning must mean something else.

But what?

Estella watched my markings pulsate; her blue eyes full of wonder.

"Your arm reminds me of something," she said, biting her lip as she considered.

"It does?"

"Yeah." She reached out to brush her fingers along my skin. The markings rippled up and down at the point of contact. I didn't feel anything unusual, but the more I looked at it, the more I got the same feeling.

I've seen this before.

Like a lightbulb turning on, Estella and I gasped at the same time, our eyes meeting as we both remembered what my markings reminded us of.

"The pool," we said at the same time.

I gripped my wrist, but the markings didn't move like they

had for Estella. I held it out, nodding my encouragement for her to try once more. Again, the markings rippled and pulsed with light. The same sort of light that had blinded me when I was in the Between.

"What pool?" Deacon and Rylan asked at the same time, their voices equally growly.

"There was a pool in the Between," I explained, looking from my arm to Estella, an idea forming. "We met in the pool."

"It always reminded me of liquid moonlight," Estella said softly, appearing dazed.

"I think I know what's wrong with Ledger." I turned back to the corner, where he was slumped. "He's trapped and needs help finding his way out."

"He's trapped in the Between?" Rylan ran a hand through his hair. "Can I guide him back like I did for you?"

It was a valid question, but we didn't even know for sure if he was in the Between to begin with. Was there a way to access that place since I'd already been there? The thought of returning made my heart skip a beat and my stomach twist. The Between wasn't a place I ever thought I would revisit, but if Ledger was there, he'd need someone to guide him back like Rylan had done with me.

"I need to go back," I murmured, the words sending a shiver down my spine.

"What? How?"

"All good questions." I wracked my brain for answers.

Was it possible to go back to the place where I was neither dead nor alive? Did I have to die again in order to go there? That thought made my stomach churn. Dying the first time was bad enough; I wasn't eager to repeat the experience.

"I was willing to do just about anything to save my cousin,

but now I'm not so sure," Rylan said honestly.

"I don't think I have to die again." I was going for reassurance, but my words just seemed to anger him more. Grey eyes turned green in an instant, and I could feel that he was moments away from grabbing me and dragging me out of here. His cousin be damned.

That wasn't right though. I knew that Rylan would choose me over his cousin in a heartbeat, but this wasn't *just* his cousin anymore. Ledger was part of the pack that we had created.

"Don't touch me," I warned him, taking a step away. I wasn't in any hurry to feel the intense burning again.

"We can try touching him," Estella suggested, wringing her hands together.

I'd bet money that she was feeling the exact same way I was about the Between. Probably stronger since she'd been there longer than I had. It wasn't a bad place. It was the thought that, while we were there, we were neither dead nor living that made me wary.

Now would have been a good time for the Moon Spirit to show up and tell us exactly what we needed to do.

I waited for a beat, crossing my fingers and praying that the Moon Spirit would hear my pleas and take pity on me. Instead, the sound of a wolf chuckling resounded in my thoughts. *You have everything you need. Trust yourself.*

Did I? All I had was a malfunctioning arm, my mate who was seconds away from locking me away, a second in command who seemed to be thinking the same thing as my mate, and Estella.

My arm ramped up in the tingling sensation, making the rest of me vibrate.

There's my sign.

Estella's suggestion about touching Ledger was as good of an idea as any to try when we didn't know what the hell we were doing. Winging it sounded good in theory, but not knowing anything else was just icing on the cake.

I took a breath in through my nose then exhaled out of my mouth. If there was a chance to save Ledger, I had to try at the very least. He didn't deserve any of this. I'd never been his biggest fan, but he was pack and part of my mate's family. I had to do this.

I stepped toward him, convinced that he would come to his senses at any moment and greet me with a sneer. He didn't react, but from the corner of my eye, I caught movement.

"Rylan," I said, warning clear in my tone.

He literally had access to my thoughts. He knew everything that I'd been thinking, and I could feel his reluctant agreement. His instincts were yelling at him to protect me, even from a pack member. This wasn't ideal, but it needed to be done. So, he could either get on board or keep quiet.

Lifting my left hand, I readied myself to place my palm on Ledger's head. Estella grabbed my other hand, her touch making my markings ripple, just like the pool had done when we shifted positions.

The closer I got to Ledger, the more intense the vibrating became. I closed my eyes, then with deliberate slowness, placed my hand on his head.

Nothing happened.

I closed my eyes tighter, expecting to feel some sort of zing or spark. Something to let me know that this craziness had worked. I waited a full minute, getting more frustrated with every second that passed. I huffed, annoyed that it wasn't working and ready to try something else.

But when I opened my eyes, I was met with darkness. I blinked, which told me that my eyes were indeed open. Everything was utter blackness.

Did it work?

It must have. I couldn't feel anything here. Even my bonds were quiet, like I'd flipped a switch and made everything pause. I wasn't in a pool, so I knew this wasn't the Between, but what else could it be?

A sinister chuckle echoed around the space, causing goosebumps to erupt on my skin. My wolf pushed forward, lending me her sight and strength. I stood frozen in place for what felt like an eternity while my heartbeat thundered in my ears. I exhaled slowly, trying to calm myself before I tried to find Estella.

Suddenly, light pulsed from my arm, giving me a quick glimpse at where I was. It appeared to be a tunnel made out of stone. The light receded, turning everything black once more.

I shook my arm, hoping that it would somehow get the light to come back on. Nothing happened. My frustration grew by the second.

My wolf scented the air. *'This doesn't smell like a cave.'*

I fought the urge to slap my forehead. We were in Ledger's head, so naturally the tunnel wouldn't smell like a normal one. I couldn't explore this place without light, so I lifted my arm and turned my thoughts to the Moon Spirit. We had a connection, and I was ninety-five percent sure that if I reached for it my arm would respond.

The markings flickered. I concentrated, filling my mind with thoughts of the Moon Spirit. I imagined it lending me its light so I could see the space around me. Slowly, my arm began to glow. After several minutes of concentration, it held a solid silvery-white light. I could see the tunnel again but there was no sign of Estella.

With deliberate steps, I walked closer to the tunnel wall. I studied its surface, confirming that it was made of stone. I looked around, finding a dead end behind me while the passage continued forward for several feet. The light from my arm could only reach a certain distance before darkness started again.

There was one way for me to continue. I took a step forward, sucking in a breath when my arm tingled pleasantly. Taking a step back, it stopped.

All right, so my markings were like a compass.

I walked forward, letting the light illuminate the space before continuing. Progress was slow, but after a few minutes of walking and nothing jumping out, my confidence grew.

I picked up my pace to a fast walk, my left arm lit up and out in front of me so I could see. The farther I walked, the cooler it became. It was subtle at first, but the temperature gradually decreased until it was definitely noticeable. That concerned me, but I wasn't entirely sure why. My wolf twitched inside of me, anxious about this place and what we could be walking into.

The tunnel made a sharp turn to the right. So far, it had been one long continuous tunnel without any curves or deviations. Pushing past my trepidation, I strolled purposely through the curved part and then stepped out of the tunnel into a massive room.

My arm didn't have enough umph to light up the room, but the lack of walls surrounding the space told me that it was definitely an open area.

My heart pounded in my chest as I hesitated, not knowing

if I should continue into the room, where I'd be vulnerable to attack, or explore the edges before moving forward.

My wolf still didn't smell anything concerning, so I took a chance and stepped out into the room. When nothing happened, I took another, then another.

Five steps later, I stopped. The edge of something reflected my light. It appeared to be made of metal, which was disconcerting since everything else had been rough stone. I drew closer, using every ounce of caution I possessed while my wolf readied herself for a fight.

The metal edges morphed into something bigger, with thick metal bars. Curious, I walked around it, finding that my suspicion was correct. It was a cage. Made to imprison a gigantic creature.

A whimpering sound reached my ears. I held my arm aloft so that I could see more of the space inside the cage. In the middle sat a boy, curled up in a ball, lying on the cold hard floor. I heard a sniffle and realized that he was crying.

My heart clenched as I took in the massive enclosure that imprisoned a small boy around the age of eight or nine, if I had to guess. I circled it again, looking for a door that would let me in, but there was nothing.

"Hey," I said quietly, not wanting to startle him. "Are you okay?"

He looked fine, dressed in clothes that appeared to be thick and warm. The boys sniffling paused when I spoke. Resting on his knees, his head moved like he was trying to get a glimpse of me.

Green irises met my gaze, and the recognition hit me like a punch to the stomach, stealing my breath away.

"Rylan?" I asked, knowing a split second later that the boy

was not my mate but someone who looked like him. "Ledger?"

The boy lifted his head, both eyes now fixed on me, a look of surprise on his face.

"Ledger, it's me, Pearl." I smiled.

"I don't know you," the boy Ledger said as the ground trembled under my feet, making my heart lurch.

"That's okay," I reassured him, keeping my voice calm and even so I didn't upset him more. "I'm a friend, and I'm here to help you."

"Help me?" he repeated, his face blank and full of confusion.

"Yes." I reached through the bars, my arm growing brighter as my heart overflowed with empathy for the small, scared boy. "I can help get you out of here."

"Can you help my friend?" He wiped his nose on the sleeve of his shirt.

"Of course," I agreed without thinking.

"Can you get him out first?"

"Uh, yeah. Where is he?" I looked around for another cage.

"He's through that doorway there." The boy pointed into the darkness behind him.

I walked around the cage until I was facing the direction the boy had indicated. I lifted my arm, sending the light from my markings into the dark space. On the very edge of where my light could reach, I saw a doorway made of stone.

Squinting, I tried to see what was in there, but the darkness was too thick for my eyes to penetrate.

Something small touched my other arm, startling me.

"You have to help him," the boy implored, his hand squeezing my arm.

"I... I'll do my best," I promised, patting his hand.

"He needs me," Ledger whispered, tears gathering in his eyes as he stared up at me.

"Don't worry. I'll find him."

Chapter Twenty-One

Pearl

I had no idea what I was looking for when I entered the second room. As soon as I stepped over the threshold, the darkness felt sinister. The fine hairs all over my body stood on end as I struggled to draw a breath through the danger that hung heavily alongside the air. My wolf squirmed under my skin, wanting to fight as much as she wanted to flee.

I raised my arm, hoping the light I possessed could displace the shadows that hung in the air like curtains. Swirls of shadow reached out like fingers, seeking the beams shining from the markings on my arm.

A deep rumble shook the floor, and I stumbled sideways, wondering what was causing these shakes. Then, I heard it. A deep chuckle rocked me to my core, it was the same one I'd heard earlier.

The sinister feeling morphed into something much darker. Violence floated through the air like fog, causing panic to bubble up and my muscles to tense.

What, or rather, *who* was chuckling?

Ledger and I had never been friends, but I never associated him with something downright evil. He always seemed high and mighty, with a swollen ego and arrogance that barely fit through the door. What I sensed now was the opposite of that.

Gathering my courage, I took a step farther into the room than another. The darkness weighed down on me like a blanket trying to suffocate me. I gritted my teeth and moved forward, determined to figure out what this was.

I lifted my arm higher, ignoring the burn from my muscles as I tried to see what was in this room.

Just when I thought there couldn't be anything here, the light glinted off of something else metal. Was it a cage? Taking a final step, I arrived at the edge of a cage that was identical to the one holding the boy in the other room. I tried to make out what was inside but didn't see anything.

Slipping my arm through the bars, I held it aloft, searching the small lit area for whatever the cage held. Something glinted in the darkness, making me stop and stare in its direction. Two round pinpoints appeared to be floating in the air. I swallowed, my heart speeding up when whatever was moved. I could barely make out the creature's outline, but I knew instantly that it was a wolf.

"Hi," I greeted it, flinching when my voice seemed to echo through the room like a gong. "The boy in the next room sent me here to… help."

I wasn't sure how I could help. The boy's cage had no discernible door or any obvious way of getting out. Instead of exploring around this cage, I decided to treat it differently.

The wolf prowled from one end to the other, making no sound except for its soft padded footsteps. I wracked my brain, trying to come up with some way to get it out of here. I had a hunch that this was Ledger's wolf. He was locked away just like the boy was.

Wrapping my hand around the cold bar made me shiver, and my arm began to burn.

This cage isn't right.

Why would there be cages in someone's mind? Both parts of Ledger were imprisoned, and I had no clue why.

"Why are you in this cage?" I wondered if Ledger had somehow created them, but I had a suspicion that this wasn't his doing.

A deep chuckle came from the darkness, and I realized it wasn't the wolf laughing but something else entirely.

"Who are you?" I asked the room, doing my best not to show how creeped out I was.

"Who are *you*?" a voice asked back, sounding oily and unnatural.

"My name's Pearl." I hoped that by answering, the voice would respond.

"The light bearer," the voice rumbled, sounding like rocks tumbling over each other. "There is nothing for you here."

"I'm not here for me." I fought a shudder.

"For the boy and his wolf?"

"Yes."

"They are mine. You cannot have them."

"What are you doing to them?" Gripping the bars, I considered whether my wolf and I were strong enough to bend them.

"I'm… caring for them." The voice paused, like it really didn't believe what it was saying.

"By putting them in separate cages in different rooms?"

"They are being punished."

"For what?" I couldn't think of any reason why the two would being punished like this.

"I was instructed to imprison both of them if the bond was severed."

"What bond?"

"The bond between mother and son."

Oh shit.

My mind started going a mile a minute, connecting the dots of the past few days. I knew that Rylan had the power to sever pack bonds; that was how he created his own pack.

This was a failsafe in case Ledger ever broke his mother's control. Anger lit a fire in my head that spread through the rest of my body.

What sort of mother could do that to her child?

Whatever this unholy darkness was, it was working for Tamra, which meant it couldn't be trusted.

"Let him go," I commanded, my voice shaking from my suppressed anger. "Let them both go."

The darkness swirled around my little bubble of light, laughing menacingly at my request. "I don't answer to you, little light bearer."

"Then, who? Tamra?"

"She is *not* my master."

I seemed to have struck a nerve. My wolf shifted uncomfortably under my skin. The sinister weight returned, making it difficult to remain upright.

"Then, who is?" I wondered, fighting to stay standing as I waited for answers.

"The blackness that lives in the shadows of shifter minds. The part of them that craves violence and power. The Moon Spirit unknowingly created its downfall when it created the Alpha Seeker. I am the end. We will rip through your kind then remake you. You will all serve the darkness, just like the witch."

What the hell?

My wolf howled, a warning that this was not somewhere we should be. She urged me to turn and run, but I couldn't. Not without Ledger and his wolf. My heart pounded in my ears, and I prayed that whatever the darkness was didn't hear it.

Frantic but not wanting to show my panic, I reached for my bonds. They were still muted, but I knew they were there. I needed help to get out of here, and last time, it was Rylan. Though, I didn't think the darkness would let me go without a fight.

My emotions overwhelmed me to the point that I was scared I'd shift and then be swallowed up by the darkness.

I need more light.

My arm pulsed, and a pressure grew inside my head that verged on pain.

"Darkness is coming, and there's nothing you can do about it."

I bit back a groan as the pressure built, pushing everything aside until it filled me so completely that I feared my head would split open. Another mind touched my thoughts, one I recognized. Rylan's presence swept through me, adding strength and support. I was able to refocus and concentrate on getting out of here.

My wolf surged forward, adding her strength to mine, and together we pushed the pressure aside. A thought occurred to me, and I searched for the source of the pressure. I felt the consciousness of the Moon Spirit and realized that it had given me access to more light. An endless supply was now open to me, and I instinctively knew that this was the solution to getting out of here alive.

I wrapped my fingers around the bars of the cage, feeling the coolness of the metal.

The cage is made of darkness.

With my wolf's help, we gathered as much light as we could through our connection with the Moon Spirit then pushed it down my left arm. Heat infused my skin as my markings began to shine brighter and brighter. The darkness pounded against the light that I was forcing into the metal.

The blackness growled around me, furious that it was losing its hold on the wolf inside the cage. The dark wolf within howled its excitement as it paced close to the bars, ready to get out. My wolf and I continued to pump light into my arm, and slowly, the bars of the cage started to fade, turning from dark metal to wispy shadows. When they were see-through, Ledger's wolf approached, swiping its leg through the lightening shadows. The residual darkness evaporated at the wolf's touch.

It was free.

Wasting no time, Ledger's wolf yipped and growled while running toward the door I'd come through earlier. Holding my arm aloft in order to keep the darkness at bay, I backtracked into the other room. Once at the entrance, I sent out a blast of brightness. The shadows scattered, withdrawing into the deep recesses of Ledger's mind.

I couldn't leave knowing there was a possibility it could corrupt him again. With the Moon Spirit's guidance, I built a barrier made of light to block the entrance to the other room. The darkness couldn't get out without hitting the wall, which would make it dissipate. It was crude and crooked, but it would have to do.

Turning, I searched for the cage that contained the boy but

found both were gone. A much older man was on the floor where the cage used to be, his arms wrapped around the wolf that I'd helped set free. The man looked up, and I saw the same eyes as the boy's staring at me from an older version his face.

"Thank you," Ledger said, emotion filling his gaze as he clung to the wolf in front of him. "We couldn't do it on our own."

"We're a pack now." I shrugged like it was no big deal.

The tunnel began to fade around us as he and his wolf became acquainted with each other. There was no telling how long they'd been separated in their own mind, but the aftermath of that sort of abuse would leave its mark on anyone. He had a long road ahead with healing and accepting what had been done to him. It wouldn't be easy, but I knew that our pack would rally and keep him safe while he worked through it.

'Time to go,' my wolf nudged me.

'How?' I didn't know how we were going to get back.

'Mate,' my wolf said, but I could hear the silent 'duh' in her words.

I reached for the bond I had with Rylan. Warmth and love enveloped me when I dipped my conscience into our connection. I closed my eyes, welcoming the feeling of my mate surrounding me. I buried myself in it, never wanting to leave this place where I belonged.

Chapter Twenty-Two

Rylan

As soon as Pearl touched my cousin's head, her body froze like she was suddenly made of stone. She wasn't breathing, and her body grew colder and colder with every passing minute that felt like an eternity.

I paced behind her and Estella, waiting for any sort of sign that they were in trouble and needed help. Estella seemed to be aware of her surroundings, plus she wasn't completely frozen like Pearl was. She still breathed and blinked, but her eyes were unfocused like she was seeing something that Deacon and I couldn't.

"What's taking so long?" Deacon growled, frustrated by the lack of any clues.

"How long have they been like this?" I made a mental note to enforce a time limit if there ever was a next time.

"Maybe ten minutes." His gaze bore into the side of Estella's head, like he could will her back just by looking at her.

"That's a long time," I murmured, approaching Pearl so I could check on her again. *No change.*

'How long will this continue for?' My wolf was just as antsy.

'Who knows.'

He didn't like my response very much but didn't say anything. I tried reaching through our bond, attempting to get any sort of sense about what was going on. The bond was silent, empty. Like Pearl had pressed pause then never returned. It was intact though, which was the only consolation I had.

Sighing, I did my best not to obsess over everything, but that was easier said than done. The truth was, I was utterly obsessed with my mate to the point of distraction. The only thing that had existed in that secret place had been us, but now, I needed to think of others.

I was ashamed to admit that I wasn't looking forward to the pack monopolizing my attention. Things were easier when it was just Pearl and me. However, I couldn't ignore the pack since I was the one who technically created it. I had a responsibility to each and every one of them. For the time being, they were safe and protected, but who knew how long it would last?

Another ten minutes went by, and my wolf was now pacing in my mind. I kept Pearl in my line of sight, my senses tuned to any changes she might make.

Without warning, all three of them gasped. I was suddenly by Pearl's side, gathering her in my arms when her body went limp. Deacon caught Estella as she too went limp. Movement in my peripheral drew my attention. Ledger's head moved sluggishly, rolling on his neck like he'd forgotten how to lift it on his own.

Pearl shivered, jerking my focus back to her. Her skin wasn't as cold as it had been, but she was definitely chilled. There was a pile of blankets by the door, so I grabbed one and tossed another to Deacon. I wrapped the warm material around my mate then squeezed her against me, sharing my body heat.

Deacon did the same thing. We needed to help them while they regained what they had lost.

"You're so warm," Pearl murmured, her head resting on my chest while her eyes blinked sleepily. "Did I do it?"

"Yes." I turned my body so she could see that Ledger was awake and looking around.

"Oh good." She let out a relieved sigh, and my chest tightened with worry.

"What happened?"

"A lot." Pearl suppressed a yawn and snuggled against me. "I'm exhausted."

"It took a toll on me last time," Estella said, her voice muffled slightly from the blanket that she was wrapped up in.

"True," Pearl agreed, and I remembered how Estella arrived then immediately fell unconscious.

"We should take them back to the house." I slid my arm under my mate's knees.

"I think that's a good idea." Deacon mirrored my movements.

"Wait. No. I have questions," Pearl protested.

"You can get them later." I stood quickly, ready to get her to a warm place.

"No, I want them now." Her persistence was endearing most of the time, but I was losing patience the more she argued.

"You need to rest first," I commanded, not taking her no as an answer.

"I can rest later." Her cheeks grew red as her chin jutted out.

"Best listen to her, cousin," Ledger chimed in, making my wolf's hackles raise.

"You shut up," I growled, not in the mood for any of his ribbing. "I'm the alpha, and it's my duty to take care of my pack."

148

CHAPTER TWENTY-TWO

"Are you going to order me to rest too?" Estella asked coolly.

I glanced at Deacon for help, but all I found was him biting his lip to keep from grinning ear to ear. *Damn him.*

"A couple of questions, then you'll rest," I conceded, mentally smiling as Pearl reluctantly agreed.

"Fine." Pearl scowled at me, but I felt through the bond that she didn't really mean it.

"Tell us what happened first." I changed the subject so she wouldn't dwell on her irritation.

"The first thing I noticed was the tunnel," Pearl began, quickly filling me and Deacon in on all that had happened inside Ledger's mind.

"That's..." Deacon trailed off, seemingly lost for words.

"I don't even know where to start," I agreed, puzzled by her explanation.

When I'd brought her and Estella back from the Between before, I remembered walking through my mind. It was dark, but there weren't any tunnels. I remembered my wolf walking beside us, my chest clenching at the thought of him or myself in cages.

I guess that was what it looked like when you'd been manipulated your whole life. As much as I disliked my cousin, I couldn't help feeling sorry for him. Had he ever had a private thought? Had my aunt controlled everything he did?

"So, light shone from your arm, showing you the way," I reiterated, concluding that it had to have been the Moon Spirit lending its light. "Tell me again about the room with the wolf in it."

Pearl repeated the story from when she stepped into the room. I couldn't make sense of who or what the voice of the darkness had been. All wolf shifters had darkness inside from the wildness of the animal we were bonded with. I could feel it in my head right this second, but it had never spoken to me. I knew from experience the urge and hunger for more power, but that was completely different from what Pearl had witnessed.

I turned to address my cousin. "Why was your wolf locked up?"

"It was a failsafe in case I ever became compromised." Ledger met my eyes and didn't flinch and looked away like most wolves would have done.

"And the plan was to... lock you and your wolf away until one or both of you died?"

"Pretty much." He shrugged, like having a dark entity inside your head holding you and your bonded hostage was normal.

"How long has it been like this?" Deacon asked the question I wasn't prepared to have answered.

"As long as I can remember. I take it from your facial expression that this isn't normal or what you have experienced?"

"Nope," Deacon and I said together.

"Interesting," Ledger mused, his eyebrows scrunched thoughtfully.

"The darkness spoke to you?" I asked Pearl, wanting to make sure that I'd heard her right.

"Yeah. It was terrifying." She shuddered, snuggling against my warm chest.

"I wonder what it could be," Deacon said as he absently rubbed Estella's back.

"I can answer that," Estella chimed in. Her face was paler than it had been, and I noticed that her hands were shaking.

A scratching sound came from the door, and I suspected it was the wolf version of Estella. The guard outside knocked before opening it a crack, which was all the invitation that the white wolf needed. She beelined for her human half, lying beside Deacon and rubbing her head on her human's shoulder then resting its head on her lap.

"I think you should rest first," Deacon interjected, looking worried.

"It can't wait." Estella shook her head. The trembling in her hands had spread to the rest of her body.

Deacon nodded, conceding quicker than I would have. He grabbed one of her hands and placed her palm over his heart, covering it with his own. Her shaking slowed as she felt his heartbeat, her breathing evening out.

"It's time I tell you all about my death."

Chapter Twenty-Three

Rylan

"Wait a second. Who is she?" Ledger asked, making everyone stop and turn toward him. "I recognize that wolf. It infuriated my mother the night of the gala."

"For good reason," Deacon retorted while the wolf bared its teeth at my cousin.

"Shhh," Estella whispered, petting the top of her wolf's head affectionately.

Shit.

How was I going to explain Estella to Ledger? I'm pretty sure he had no idea that his mother murdered her only sister.

"Sorry," I muttered, clearing my throat before glancing at Estella, who nodded her head in permission. "This is Estella... your aunt."

No one said anything for a beat, then he threw his head back and laughed. Everyone stared at him as he continued for nearly a full minute. When no one else joined in, he got a clue that this wasn't at all humorous.

"What are you saying?" Ledger swallowed hard as he took in the serious faces of everyone in the room.

"Estella is your mother's sister," Pearl said without a trace of humor in her tone.

"That's not… how is this possible?"

"Let her tell her story, and maybe you'll learn," Deacon gritted out, his jaw muscles flexing as his anger grew.

Estella leaned her head against his chest, and I saw the anger and frustration drain out of him by her simple touch. I'd suspected before, but now I was sure that my friend had found his mate. It made me happy that he had found his person, but it also worried me.

Estella was not like normal shifters. She had been separated from her wolf when Tamra killed her. She was essentially split into two different beings, her human half and her animal side. Since she was fully human, could she bond with her mate in the usual way? Would Deacon be able to get what he needed without a traditional bond? There was no way of knowing, and it hurt my heart to picture him without the mate bond like Pearl and I had.

Now was not the time to be wondering about that though. When the time came, I would do everything in my power to help the two of them. Their bond might not have been normal, but neither was mine and Pearl's. We just had to cross that bridge when we got to it.

Judging by the look on Deacon's face, I knew it wasn't going to be easy, but like me, he was strong and ready for whatever obstacles were in his way.

"Tamra is older than me. She was bright, talented, and smart. I remember growing up, admiring her and hoping that I'd be just like her." A sad smile lifted the corners of Estella's lips, and I understood that look all too well. "Everything changed when she met her mate, who was a rogue passing through the valley. He didn't want a mate and rejected her. Tamra took the rejection hard. She withdrew into herself, finding solace in her own mind instead of reality.

"I remember going to visit her and overhearing her talking to someone. At first, I thought it was her wolf, but she was speaking out loud. I thought it strange but ignored it, telling myself this was all part of the healing process. She grew more and more distant as time went on. My parents worried that her mate's rejection would be the end of her. There was nothing we could do but wait, hope, and pray.

"One day, a man around her age stopped by our home to pick up something from my father. It was the alpha's second son, Bear. He was strapping, capable, and gorgeous. There was a magnetic aura around him that appealed to both humans and wolves. There were many females who had a crush on him, me included. He was nice and easy to talk to. I remember feeling envious of whoever his mate would turn out to be.

"Unknowingly, that day, Bear had caught the attention of my sister. She returned from whatever dark place she had been in. There was vibrancy back in her eyes, and I thought her depression was good and truly over. Until her infatuation became an obsession. She was determined to win his heart by being the very best alpha female who could stand at a strong alpha's side.

"It worked for a time, but Bear's attention would wander, always searching for his mate. Then, one day, he found her."

"Faela," Pearl breathed, totally enraptured by the story.

"Yes. She was the Alpha Seeker and protected by her family. She had never been revealed to the packs, but when she turned eighteen, it was time. Both families were overjoyed that they were mates. Bear would become the next great alpha, with Faela by his side. When Tamra heard of this, she became so angry."

"I can understand that. She'd convinced herself that Bear was her mate," Deacon interjected, while Pearl and I nodded our agreement.

"Tamra became... volatile," Estella whispered, squeezing her eyes shut like it had just happened yesterday.

"That's an understatement," I grumbled, remembering the research I had done into Faela and her history.

"To this day, I'm still not sure how she was able to nearly erase Faela from memory. I know Faela was sent to prison and her family died from mysterious circumstances. Bear was grief stricken, but there wasn't much he could do. Through it all, Tamra was there for him, biding her time.

"Tamra became edgy and violent. She wouldn't leave Bear's side, and that's when things went downhill. Bear's older brother, Wolf, wasn't nearly powerful enough to overthrow his father. On the day Wolf issued the challenge, my sister revealed that she was pregnant. The whole pack's attention landed on my sister, and our parents demanded that they mate. With great reluctance, Bear took my sister as his mate."

"This is the opposite of a romantic story," Pearl grumbled, and I had to agree with her. Manipulation and coercion were not a good foundation for mating.

"Shush," Ledger hissed, but it didn't have his normal attitude behind it.

"The pregnancy was a lie," Estella revealed. "Tamra reached out to me and asked for my help. I loved my sister, so I agreed. We staged a fake miscarriage, which messed with Bear's mind. He became suspicious and demanding. He was obsessed with the thought of having a child, to the point where he was ready to partition the pack for a second mate. That's when my sister lost her sanity."

"Can't blame her." I didn't want to feel sympathy toward my aunt, but I could empathize with her pain. I'd lose my mind if Pearl went to someone else for her needs. The thought alone had red hot fury coursing through my veins.

"Worried about my sister and wanting to help, I went to the Cage and visited Faela. She was in good spirits, regardless of her incarceration. She was kind and felt pity for my sister, who just wanted someone to love her. I vowed to help my sister anyway I could. So, I offered Bear and Tamra my body. I'd carry a child for them with the hope that it would heal their damaged hearts and bring them together again."

"My sister didn't appreciate my offer. She became jealous and overbearing, even cruel. She refused my offer then tried to manipulate those around her, so she had support when she approached her mate and the alpha, asking them to banish me."

"It was too much. I withdrew my offer and hid away, hoping that by staying out of sight, my presence wouldn't insight her ire. I was wrong though. My absence seemed to further push her toward madness.

"Tamra came to me one night, asking for assistance. Like a fool, I followed her without question. She led me to a rocky area high up in the mountains. There was no moon in the sky, which should have been a hint, but I was so desperate to have my sister back that I ignored the warning signs until it was too late."

The chains still restraining my cousin clinked together as he sat forward, his greenish eyes, much like mine, never leaving Estella's face.

"Tamra attacked me with no provocation. I collapsed, and my wolf did everything she could to heal the wound, but it was too severe. My sister had stabbed my heart. We fought for our life, but then Tamra called on the darkness and it answered her. She offered me as a sacrifice to the darkness in order to gain enough power to conquer every wolf, every pack. The darkness lapped at my blood, using the Moon Spirit's power flowing through my veins to transform. A wolf made entirely of shadows manifested before us, its eyes empty of emotion but full of malice.

"I remember my sister watching without remorse as the wolf tore open my chest and ate my heart. During my last breaths, the Moon Spirit entered my mind, blocking out the pain and fear. She asked us not to fight but to instead trust her. With no other option, we surrendered to the Moon Spirit, not the Shadow Wolf that had been born that night. I was sent to the Between, a place of limbo where you are neither living nor dead, to wait for the right time to return and help destroy my sister. My wolf remained here, watching and waiting for the correct moment.

"The Moon Spirit kept her promise. I returned to this life and have been reunited with my wolf, but we are not the same and never will be again."

Chapter Twenty-Four

Pearl

My heart ached for Estella and her wolf. She'd been through something horrific all while trying to help her ungrateful sister. I couldn't imagine what she must have felt during those final moments, but I was happy that the Moon Spirit intervened. She didn't deserve any of what happened. All to heal her sister's heart, who then took hers and gave it to an evil entity.

I couldn't fathom how she was able to accept it all. I supposed by the promise that she would one day be united with her wolf again. Judging by the grip that Deacon had on her, the Moon Spirit had blessed her with a mate too. I didn't know really Deacon, but by observing him with Estella, I knew that the Moon Spirit had chosen well. They were meant for each other, though I wasn't sure if either of them was aware of it yet.

"I don't know what to say." My heart was broken for Estella and her wolf. They'd been dealt a horrible hand; one I couldn't imagine ever coming back from. I admired her bravery and courage. Knowing her story made me appreciate her presence all the more.

"We can't change the past." Estella turned so she could see

Deacon's face. "I've been given a second chance. I'm not going to waste it."

Deacon leaned his head down until their foreheads touched, their eyes drinking each other in. My chest warmed at the affectionate display. I wished them all the luck in the world.

"Your story makes me understand my mother a bit more." Ledger frowned, his head falling back against the wall behind him. "That doesn't excuse her actions."

"No. It seems like she upped her game once the Alpha Seeker escaped from prison and a new one was appointed," Rylan added, his brows furrowed as he tightened his hold on me.

"She thought Faela's death was the end until she realized there was a new Alpha Seeker. The Moon Spirit was cunning. As far as we knew, the Alpha Seeker title was always inherited, not bestowed." Ledger's voice was soft, but I could hear his pain in every word he spoke.

"What are your thoughts on all of this?" Rylan directed his question at his cousin, and I could sense through our bond that he didn't want to hope that Ledger was on our side now.

Ledger's lips twisted while his chest rumbled a growl that I'm sure his wolf was dying to let out. "She may be my mother, but she's manipulated me and my father for years. Not to mention all of the other lives she's ruined, plus bringing a Shadow Wolf to life." He shook his head and bit his lip, as if fighting back emotions. "She's too far gone."

"So, you agree that she must be stopped, no matter the cost?" Rylan asked the burning question everyone was thinking. Was Ledger on our side now?

"I never had a choice before, but now that I'm free of her manipulations and the darkness she let fester inside of me, I'm ready to say that she must be stopped. I don't care how."

"I'm glad to know that you are on our side," Rylan replied, but I could feel that he wasn't entirely sold on the fact that his cousin would stand with us. It was his family, after all, and blood was thicker than a pack. We'd just have to wait and see what happened.

I'd been inside of his head and felt that terrifying darkness that did its best to corrupt my light. It wouldn't let go so easily. The threats it made still echoed through my thoughts, making my stomach clench with unease.

We will rip through your kind and remake you.

I didn't know what it meant by 'remake', but from the burning sensation in my arm and the way my heart thudded in my ears, it couldn't have been good. For any of us.

A yawn took me by surprise, my jaw popping as it overtook me. My eyes grew heavy, and I knew that if I didn't get to bed soon, I would fall asleep right here.

"I think that's our cue," Estella said, stifling her own yawn. "Let's go back to the house and rest."

I nodded, too tired to form words.

"You two go on ahead." Deacon helped Estella to her feet and held on to her until she was steady. "We've got more to discuss but will be along soon."

"All right." I yawned again, snuggling closer to Rylan's chest, soaking in his warmth for as long as I could.

"I'll come with you," he announced, squeezing me tightly.

"No, I've got her. Let's go, friend." Estella took my arm to better support me while her wolf stood pressed against her other side.

'I love you,' Rylan whispered in my mind, making me grin like a schoolgirl with her first crush.

'I love you more,' I countered in a teasing tone.

CHAPTER TWENTY-FOUR

Rylan mock growled in my head, and I chuckled.

'Don't be too long.'

'Don't tell me what to do,' he shot back, but I knew full well that he liked it when I told him what to do.

Thinking of all the sexy situations we'd been in due to me telling him exactly what to do made my mouth salivate. There would be time for more of that soon enough.

Estella opened the door to the cellar, and the cool air slapped me in the face, pushing my exhaustion away just a tad. The door closed behind us, and we both took a deep breath, looking up at the stars that littered the dark sky above. After what I'd been through in Ledger's head, the darkness didn't hold much appeal anymore, but I tried to enjoy it regardless. I was the Alpha Seeker, and I wouldn't let our enemy taint what I enjoyed.

'That's the spirit,' my wolf said, fighting her own exhaustion. 'With Ledger on our side, I think the tables have finally tilted in our favor.'

'We'll see.' She didn't sound convinced.

'What's up?'

'I just feel like there's more going on than we realize. I can't pinpoint why I feel like this, but I'm expecting a shoe to drop at any moment.'

I frowned, trying to get my sluggish mind to speed up so I could figure out why she was feeling this way. From the beginning, I felt like there was more going on than just Tamra wanting to control all of the packs. Discovering the darkness had helped the puzzle pieces fall into place, but maybe I was missing something else. Tamra had control of the packs at the moment, except for our small one. What more could she want?

My wolf was right. There had to be more to everything that

161

she was doing and had done in the past. What was her end game?

The crossroads that the Moon Spirit revealed to me popped up in my mind from the night everything was revealed to me. The left path was extinction, the universe's way of righting the unbalance with our species. The right, safer option was *near* extinction. Neither one was great, but was the universe ready to take that sort of drastic measure?

The Moon Spirit thought so, and that had to be enough for me. For now.

Estella and I were halfway to the cabin when a sudden chill ran down my spine, followed by a decrease in temperature. We both stopped, looking around the area for any sort of danger. My wolf was alert, ready to push forward and protect us from whatever the threat was.

Estella's wolf let out a low warning growl, making my muscles tense.

What was going on?

Instinctively, I reached for Rylan to alert him that something wasn't right out there, but my thoughts ran into a wall that cut off our bond. My heart lurched, panic bubbling up inside me when I couldn't reach him. My wolf rammed against the mental barrier, but it didn't budge.

Rustling from the shadows drew all of our attention. Estella's wolf moved between us and the shadows, her teeth bared and a growl rattling her chest. A figure stepped out of the darkness, and a second later, one became two.

Estella's white wolf in front of us charged, but the first figure backhanded her, causing her to fly backward and hit the ground with an audible whine. Estella dropped my arm and rushed toward her wolf but was intercepted by the second figure.

The first grabbed me before I could help. Its icy touch made me shiver. My arm burned, and I thought it might combust. Darkness pressed in around me, and my arm hung uselessly at my side. I tried to summon the light like I had in Ledger's mind, but nothing happened.

Terror slammed into me when a deep chuckle sounded from the darkness. I'd already heard that voice tonight.

I opened my mouth to scream, but a cold hand wrapped around my throat, the fingers squeezing, cutting off the sound before I could get it out.

"We meet again, my little moonbeam."

Chapter Twenty-Five

Rylan

I took off the chains binding my cousin to the wall, thankful that he hadn't broken free, even though he could have easily done so.

"Now that the girls are gone," I said, watching as Ledger rubbed his wrists, "is there anything I should know about?"

"Are you asking if I know what my mother is planning?" Ledger asked bluntly.

"Yes."

"You're in luck. I know part of the plan, but not all of it. Mother is particular about who knows what."

"Has she always manipulated you?" I couldn't help but ask. If so, it would explain everything.

"Yes, but only a little bit in the beginning. It got worse the older I grew. Then, when the Alpha Seeker escaped the Cage, she ramped it up to a whole other level. I remember feeling the intense urge to protect the Gala at all costs. I had to plan for every contingency. Looking back, it was strange, even for her, but then shit hit the fan and everything started to make sense. She needed to ensure another Alpha Seeker didn't show up and ruin her plans to take full control."

"Why did she send you *and* Alder?"

"If Alder failed, I was supposed to step in and finish the job. She knew you had the power to release wolves from her control after the Gala incident; she just didn't know how."

"So, Alder was a decoy, basically."

"Basically." He shrugged, and I hated how nonchalant he was.

"What was your plan after that?"

"Take you down. I was ordered to kill you if given the chance. I underestimated your abilities, especially in your partial-beast form. It takes energy and concentration to maintain that sort of shift, but you handled it just fine." Ledger raised his eyebrows in question, but I bit my cheek, refusing to explain.

The truth was, I wasn't entirely sure how I'd managed to maintain the partial form for so long, but I suspected it was because of my wolf. Both of us working together were able to hold our form while fighting, which, until then, was completely unheard of.

My wolf huffed his agreement. It hadn't always been an easy road for us, but we'd pushed through. Now, we were here— alpha of our own pack and mated to the Alpha Seeker, which meant we would unite the packs.

'One step at a time,' my wolf admonished in a gruff voice.

Speaking of the Alpha Seeker, I reached for Pearl through our bond and found it completely quiet. Had she fallen asleep that quickly? She'd only left a couple minutes ago, but maybe she'd been able to avoid Arden and go straight to bed.

I tried to shrug it off, but a nagging part of me was convinced that something wasn't right.

"Everything okay?" Deacon asked, watching me intently. He was always good at reading my body language.

"It's nothing. The bond with Pearl is just quiet."

"Could she be asleep?"

"Yeah, it happened really fast..." I trailed off, reaching through the bond again and finding nothing there.

My wolf squirmed uneasily, also picking up on the strangeness.

"I need to go make sure she's okay." I thought we were ready, but maybe we should have stayed in our secret place for longer. I couldn't be the alpha my pack needed if I was obsessing over my mate all the time.

The urge to see her and make sure she was all right grew with every passing second. I stormed to the door and wrenched it open, nearly ripping the whole thing off of its hinges. Taking a breath, I found my mate's scent in the air, telling me she had walked through this area recently.

Heading down the path, I didn't bother to see if Deacon or my cousin were following. I was sure they were.

Halfway between the cellar and the cabin, her scent disappeared. I backtracked, wondering if her and Estella had turned around to return, but there was no indication that they had changed direction.

Panic started to build in my chest, but the logical side of me was trying to think rationally. A scent trail didn't just disappear into thin air without a reason.

A frustrated growl rumbled through my chest as I ran through every possibility. Pearl and Estella had definitely come this way, but now they were gone.

"Do you smell that?" I asked Deacon, who was standing to my right.

"Yeah," he confirmed, his own frustration clear in his voice.

"Where'd they go?" Ledger murmured from my left side.

I called on my wolf sight and studied the grass. There were two distinct sets of footsteps. They continued for a couple more feet before they disappeared entirely. I backed up, retracing their steps again, praying that I was missing something. But I came to the same conclusion as before.

"We should go search the cabin just in case," Deacon suggested, already making his way toward the building.

"Don't bother." Ledger stood off to the side, his hands outstretched. "They're both gone."

"Gone? Gone where?" Deacon demanded, but I could sense the answer.

"They've been taken."

"What? How?"

"If I had to guess, I'd say it was the shadows." Ledger waved his hand through the air, causing some sort of disturbance.

"What the fuck is that?" Deacon's grip on his control was slipping.

"The darkness took them," Ledger answered, moving his fingers in the lingering shadows. "The Shadow Wolf left this as a calling card. Somehow, he snatched the girls without leaving anything to trace."

"Where would he take them?" My question was a growl full of unfiltered fury.

"My guess is to her." His shoulders drooped in defeat.

"What could she possibly want with them?" Deacon growled; his tone was dangerous. If there was any doubt before, there wasn't any now. Estella was Deacon's mate, and the fact that she'd been taken was making him see red. Much like I was.

"Estella shouldn't have survived. The fact that she did probably made mother curious, and Pearl... I think she took her to get to you." Ledger looked me in the eye when he said the last part.

This was a direct attack on me. Somehow, she knew that Pearl and I had completed the mate bond. She also knew that her sister wasn't dead, as she had once believed. This was Tamra's second attack in a matter of days, which meant she was confident we weren't a threat.

That wasn't true though. I was an alpha now, and I would not roll over or abandon any of my pack members. Tamra was banking on that.

She was drawing me out and using the Shadow Wolf and my mate to do it, which was low, even for her. I wouldn't let her get away with it. If she wanted a fight so badly, then I'd give her just that.

Chapter Twenty-Six

P earl

I coughed, trying to dispel the thick cloying darkness that had surrounded Estella, her wolf, and me. The ground fell away, and I panicked for a split second before our feet slammed into the hard ground. My knees buckled, and I fell forward, teeth gritted against the pain. Estella was on the ground beside me, a similar look of panic and pain written on her face. Her wolf growled deep and menacing.

Glancing around, I tried to figure out where we were while simultaneously reaching for my mate bond. Emptiness greeted me. Anger and fear coursed through my veins, making me pray for my mate's safety to the Moon Spirit. Whatever this was, I needed Rylan to be all right. I could handle whatever came my way, but if he was hurt or something worse, my wolf and I would tear this place down.

"Where are we?" Estella asked, her voice shaky but quiet.

"I'm not sure," I replied, but after my perusal, I had the nagging feeling that I'd been here before.

'We have. This is Faela's cell.'

I suppressed my gasp of recognition, not wanting to give anything away. Our captors were no doubt watching us. Better not to reveal that I knew where we were. Not yet at least.

"Well, well, well," a condescending female voice echoed around the room.

I glanced around, but saw no one but us, which made me frown. Where was the voice coming from?

Estella's white wolf lifted her jowls in a snarl, placing herself between the threat and her human half. I followed the wolf's line of sight, forgetting that Faela's cell was in the Cage and the opening was in the ceiling.

"I can honestly say that I didn't think I'd ever see you again." Tamra chortled, her gaze roaming over her sister. "The Moon Spirit must have been looking out for you all along."

Estella didn't say anything, just lifted her chin, glaring at her sister who had done her best to kill her. Her wolf bared her teeth, an obvious challenge that Tamra ignored.

"I'll be sure to do it right next time," Tamra promised, the evil gleam in her eye pointing to the dark power she'd killed for. "Killing you again will be the cherry on top, after I finish with your friend."

Her gaze moved to me, and like a switch had been flipped, my left arm started to burn, and light emanated from my markings.

"The light show is new," she mused, watching me with a sort of hunger in her eyes that gave me the creeps.

What was the bitch planning?

"I'm sure your mate knows you've been taken by now." She seemed excited about the prospect.

I bit the inside of my cheek to keep from commenting. She didn't deserve any type of response from me, plus I didn't want to give anything away. I checked the bond and found that nothing had changed. I could only imagine the state Rylan was in right now knowing I'd been taken. I wished I could reassure him that I was all right; doing so would probably help him not do something stupid.

"Get comfortable, pets. It's nearly time."

"Time for what?" Estella asked me quietly once Tamra had disappeared from the opening in the ceiling.

"I have no idea." I reached through the bond again, hoping that something had changed.

Glancing around the room, I searched for something that might have been blocking my connection to Rylan, but nothing immediately jumped out.

Estella shivered, and belatedly, I remembered that she was entirely human. Her wolf couldn't help keep her warm, and it was obvious that her wolf was annoyed by it. The white wolf patted the stone floor with her paw while staring at her human half. Taking the hint, Estella sat down with her back against the wall as her wolf lay across her lap.

I paced around the room, using all my senses to hopefully find something I could use. Maybe I could call another bone from the wall and use it as a club like I did with Rylan.

It feels like ages since I've been here.

The reality was it had only been a couple weeks. The cavernous cell hadn't changed, and I felt like if I wasn't able to breath in fresh air soon, I'd go mad.

'*Try reaching for the Moon Spirit,*' my wolf suggested.

I tried, reaching out to the universe around me, but there was no reply.

"Come sit." Estella patted the stone beside her.

"Do you have any ideas?" My skin crawled from the loss of the mate bond. "I can't reach Rylan."

"I've got a couple theories, but the most important thing we need to figure out now is how to unblock your bond with

Rylan. He's our only hope."

I took a deep breath, calming the raging emotions that coursed through me making my chest tight.

I swallowed and nodded. Sitting down beside her, I forced my body to relax as best as I could. Once I was settled and breathing evenly, I tried to reach through the bond again. This time there was a glimmer of awareness. I could feel Rylan's anger and heard a couple mumbled words that didn't make sense before I was cut off again.

Estella listened as I told her what had just happened, a frown on her pretty face. "Try again but close your eyes and push everything aside as much as you can."

I did what she suggested, closing my eyes and slowing my breathing before I reached through the bond once more. More mumbled words, an angry shout, and Rylan's red rage.

"I think the bond is blocked by the darkness that resides in Rylan. That's what the Shadow Wolf is, after all. The more he rages, the further the bond is pushed away." Estella explained.

"How do I stop it?" I wondered, anxious about the darkness I'd felt in Ledger being in my mate too.

"You need to be completely relaxed. Here, lay down and put your head on my lap."

I was willing to try just about anything at this point.

I lay on my side, my head resting on Estella's thigh, her wolf's fur mixing with my own hair. Running her fingers through my hair, Estella tried to help me calm down.

"The darkness is blocking the bond from Rylan's side. If you relax your mind enough, you might be able to find a way in without alerting the Shadow Wolf. Close your eyes and let the exhaustion you are feeling pull you into sleep."

I closed my eyes and relaxed my body, letting the exhaustion that I felt deep in my bones take over. With Estella's fingers on my scalp and her wolf's steady breathing, I fell into the darkness that tugged at my mind, hoping that I would be able to reach my mate.

Something jerked at my consciousness. I snapped my eyes open and looked around. I was still in Faela's cell, but now I was sitting in the middle of the cavern with my legs crossed. I couldn't see Estella or her wolf anywhere, which made my heartbeat faster.

"What..." I got out then turned back around, gasping when I saw an old woman sitting across from me.

"Hello, Pearl," the apparition greeted me.

I swallowed thickly and pinched my thighs, trying to determine if I was dreaming or not.

"This is a dreamscape," the older woman said with a hint of amusement in her voice. "You are dreaming but also aware of this."

"What do you want?" I reached for my wolf. She was there but not reacting to the strangeness that was currently going on.

"Don't you recognize me?" A corner of the woman's mouth lifted as she smirked.

Now that she mentioned it, she did look familiar.

"Faela?" My eyes widened as I looked at her with new understanding.

"Yes." She chuckled good naturally.

"What's going on? How are you here?"

"I'm still dead, but the Moon Spirit and I agreed that it would be best for me to speak to you," Faela began then shifted, like she was trying to get into a more comfortable position. "I know everything that has happened, and I know where you are right now. Being in my cell has allowed my spirit to reach out to yours. We can speak freely here."

I nodded, a million questions running through my mind. There was so much I wanted to know and questions that didn't have answers, but I didn't want to waste this time with the previous Alpha Seeker. I didn't know how long this would last, so I'd better make every moment count.

"Do you know... what's going to happen to me?"

"You are going through a... transformation." *She took a moment to look around at the place that had been her prison for decades.* "Being held here was miserable, but it gave me what I needed. Time. The Moon Spirit never abandoned me. We spoke daily, and not too long ago, we started planning."

"Planning what?"

"I'll tell you, but you've got to shut up and listen," *Faela snapped, the tranquility she was going for forgotten in a split second.* "You know as well as I do what the repercussions of the universe are. Balance must be restored, and it will do that by any means necessary, even side with the enemy. The Moon Spirit and I discussed every possible outcome from the most likely to the everything-went-to-shit. In every scenario, we came to the same conclusion. In order to restore balance, the Moon Spirit must die."

"Um, excuse me?" *I giggled, fighting a manic episode that began clouding my mind.* "The Moon Spirit is a god. Gods can't be killed."

"The Moon Spirit created this mess. In order to fix it, it needs to sacrifice itself for the betterment of everyone."

"No. No, no, no. This can't be happening."

The Moon Spirit was the only being who would stand a chance against the Shadow Wolf. How does a sacrifice lead to balance? I couldn't wrap my head around what the old wolf was talking about.

"The universe needs its pound of flesh, a sacrifice, and it'll accept only the Moon Spirit," *Faela continued, ignoring my outburst.* "In order to save everyone, the Moon Spirit will surrender to Tamra."

174

"Why? There has to be another way." Tears welled in my eyes at the thought of a world without the Moon Spirit in it.

"There isn't, I'm afraid." Faela appeared just as upset as I felt. "I wish there was another way, but there isn't."

"What happens after that? Will Tamra gain more power? Take the Moon Spirit's place?" No one knew what Tamra was after, not even her son.

The look on Faela's face told me the answer.

"Tamra intends to become the Moon Spirit?" That couldn't be possible.

"The Shadow Wolf has opened Tamra's eyes to all sorts of possibilities. She aims to become a goddess, a being of both light and dark."

"That won't fix the balance issue," I grumbled.

"No, it won't. Which is why we, the Moon Spirit and I, have come up with an alternative."

"What's the alternative?" I couldn't see how they were going to prevent this from happening. Tamra was too powerful.

"You," Faela whispered, her eyes growing misty, which was more alarming than what she'd just said.

"Wait... me?"

"The transference has already started. The Moon Spirit is passing its powers to you."

"To me?"

My left arm tingled, drawing my attention down to it. The markings covering it glowed with an inner light that reminded me of moonlight.

I thought light coming from my arm was just another Alpha Seeker perk, but I was transitioning.

"What does this mean? Will I become the Moon Spirit?"

"In a way. You will have abilities and duties that you must

perform, but you will not *be a god. You will live a normal life."*

"Will the powers be passed on or will they die with me?"

"That's a question only you can answer," Faela said unhelpfully.

Great.

"What about Rylan?"

"He has his own path to walk."

"What does that mean?"

"It means he'll be faced with a similar decision, one that only he can make. Stopping Tamra is top priority. The Moon Spirit's power can only be wielded by it or you."

"What if she succeeds?"

"Then, all is lost."

No fucking pressure.

"There isn't much time. Tamra's coming for you. She will try to weaken you. Hold on for as long as you can."

"Wait, what does that mean?"

"I'm going to open the bond you have with Rylan. You're going to need his strength."

"Faela, wait. Please. I have more questions," I pleaded with the old woman, but her eyes filled with sadness.

"This is the only time I was allowed. I couldn't have picked a more worthy person to inherit my Alpha Seeker powers. You'll do amazing things, Pearl."

With those final words, the cavern and Faela began to fade. I tried to hold on, needing more time, but there was nothing I could do. The more I held on, the faster the room and the old lady disappeared.

I was alone again in the darkness of my mind. Grief and weariness weighed heavily on my shoulders while my left arm gradually began to brighten, pushing the darkness aside.

"Pearl!"

Chapter Twenty-Seven

Rylan

'*Rylan.*' Pearl's voice whispered through my mind. I closed my eyes, letting her presence soothe me and my wolf.

Instinctively, I reached into her mind, making sure she wasn't injured or harmed in any way. What I found was that my mate was sad and… grieving? My thoughts went immediately to Estella. Was she hurt?

I wrapped my conscientiousness around Pearl, offering comfort as her sadness flooded my senses. I was able to piece together that Estella and her wolf were fine and that all three of them were in relative safety.

For the first time since they'd been taken, I was able to relax. Knowing Pearl was safe went a long way to calming me. My hands had partially shifted, my claws biting into my palms as I tried relentlessly to break through whatever was blocking our bond.

'*Pearl? Baby, what's wrong? Talk to me,*' I begged her, needing verbal confirmation that she was all right.

'*We're okay,*' she replied, but the way she said it made me think that the opposite was true.

'Do you know where you are?' Hopefully, she hadn't been taken somewhere she didn't recognize.

'The Cage,' Pearl said, making my wolf's hackles raise at the thought of our precious mate in that horrible place. *'We're in Faela's cell.'*

I wondered briefly why Tamra would take them there, but since I wasn't insane, I thought it best not to try to make sense of it.

'All right, I'm grabbing some wolves and we'll be there soon.'

'No, you need to bring everyone.'

'I can't bring everyone. I'm not sure if being part of my pack will protect the wolves' minds from Tamra's control.'

'It will,' she assured me.

I gripped my hair in my hands, the pain in my scalp a welcome distraction. *'How do you know?'*

'I just do. You have to trust me, Rylan.'

I did trust her, but I knew that if the opportunity presented itself, Pearl would sacrifice herself to save others. My mate was selfless, and while it was an admirable trait for an alpha female, it made me and my wolf antsy.

'Promise me you won't do anything reckless.' I needed to hear her say that she'd protect herself until I got to her.

'Reckless? Me?' she snipped, some of her spunk coming back, making me feel less anxious. *'I'll do my best.'*

I knew that was all I was going to get from her, so I let the subject go.

Deacon's wolf huffed his annoyance as he paced the living room. Shortly after we realized that Pearl and Estella had been taken, he'd shifted into his wolf form. He was agitated, and it was taking more energy than I liked to keep him here. If I'd let him, he would have run off in search of Estella and would have walked right into a trap or worse.

I had no doubt in my mind that this was Tamra's impatience. She had always hated waiting, so she'd stolen the two wolves we would do just about anything to draw us out. Gritting my teeth, I tried to think rationally.

'Do you know what she is planning?' I asked Pearl gently. She still seemed volatile, and I didn't want to upset her more.

'I think so.' Pearl's response was quiet, telling me that she knew more than she was saying. But I couldn't demand answers from her. She was my equal in every way, and if she was keeping something from me, I knew in my gut there was a reason. Didn't mean I liked it though.

"Estella is okay," I said to the still-pacing wolf.

The outline of Deacon's wolf blurred at the edges as his form shifted and changed into that of a naked human. Ledger tossed him some sweatpants that he hurriedly pulled on. His movements were shaky, which wasn't like him at all. He was usually the level-headed one, but I guess finding one's mate threw all control out the window.

"Where are they?" His voice was deep and growly, and I knew his wolf was close to the surface. I couldn't blame him for his reaction. Hell, it took everything I had not to let my wolf charge off on his own. We needed to be smart about this.

Tamra wouldn't try to lure me out for no reason. She was planning something, and I had a feeling it had to do with Pearl, and through her, me. She had to be stopped. Her path to more power was paved with blood and darkness.

'Someone's here. I have to wake up now.'

'Wait!' I yelled, surging toward the bond to keep it from closing.

I was too late. Pearl was gone, and our bond was once again

silent.

"She's gone," I gritted out, black fur starting to sprout from my arms as my control slipped.

"Where are they?" Deacon asked again. His eyes darted around wildly.

I had to act before he did something stupid. "They're in the Cage." I reached out and grabbed my beta wolf by the shoulders. "You need to keep it together, man."

"We need a plan," Ledger cut in, ignoring the annoyed growl from Deacon.

"Why the Cage?" Deacon glared at Ledger, who didn't even flinch.

"It must be important somehow."

"Estella said she went to a place high on the mountain to meet her sister before she died," Ledger rubbed his chin absently. "Didn't she mention rocks?"

"What the fuck do rocks have to do with anything?" Deacon snarled, fur beginning to appear all over his chest and shoulders.

"Because... there's a place near an entrance to the Cage that's rocky," Ledger murmured as he began to pace the same path that Deacon had been earlier. "It's the same way Faela escaped, which means something to my mother."

"She can't be that sentimental." I scoffed, never having gotten the impression that my aunt cared.

"She's not, but that's also the place where her initial plan with Estella failed. I'd bet my life that my mother is planning to go there."

"How sure are you?" I asked, before sharing a quick look with Deacon.

"Very sure."

"Let's send a scout first. Teo?"

The big Enforcer wolf grunted from the kitchen while speaking to one of his wolves.

"Check in when you get there."

"Now what?" Deacon flexed his arm and chest muscles like he was hyping himself up for a fight.

"Do you have any theories as to what she might be planning?" I asked my cousin.

"From what I've witnessed and seen, I don't think she's satisfied with the amount of power that she has. At the Gala, you ripped through her control, easily freeing other wolves."

"She wants more power. Why?"

What more could she possibly want?

"Think about it. She had no control over anything in her life. This power from the Shadow Wolf gives her control but only a small amount. If I had to guess, I'd say that Mother wants to be the most powerful creature in the universe."

"How does one do that though?" Deacon frowned and gripped his hands into fists.

"A sacrifice," Ledger answered quietly. "She's going to need a sacrifice. She's already used her sister. I wonder what sort of power the Moon Spirit would grant her if she threatened the Alpha Seeker."

My eyes grew wide as my brain registered what he was saying. Tamra was going to sacrifice Pearl to the Shadow Wolf in exchange for power from the Moon Spirit. With control of both the light and the dark, no one would be able to stop her.

It was a terrifying thought. One that I couldn't just sit by and let happen. My mate would not be my aunt's sacrifice.

Not if I could help it.

Chapter Twenty-Eight

P earl

I started to wake up, but I wasn't ready to face what I knew was coming. I couldn't even tell Rylan. He was my mate. The other half of my soul... but I couldn't find the words or the courage to tell him.

If he figured out where Tamra was, he was going to be so pissed.

Consciousness called to me, and with reluctance I opened my eyes. Darkness greeted me, and for a moment, I thought I might still be asleep, but then I felt the arms around me. Alarmed, I squirmed, trying to get away from whoever was carrying me.

'It's all right,' my wolf assured me, having been completely aware of what was going on around us. *'We're being taken to Tamra.'*

'Where's Estella?'

'She's walking behind with her wolf. We tried to wake you, but you refused.'

I gulped, the reality of the situation coming to the forefront of my mind making me tremble. This next part was completely unknown, and I was terrified. For my pack. For Rylan and

Estella. And for me.

This was the next obstacle I had to overcome as the Alpha Seeker, but I wasn't ready for any of it. Faela had explained, but there were things that we couldn't predict, which made my stomach churn. How was I going to handle all of this? Or stop Tamra from doing what she was going to attempt?

I didn't know, so I did what I'd always done when faced with a difficult decision—I reached for the Moon Spirit. The white wolf responded immediately. No matter what happened, I knew I wouldn't be alone.

'Are you ready for this?' I asked my wolf, needing to hear her opinion.

'We'll be fine. The Moon Spirit wouldn't do this if it thought there was another way. We need to trust them."

Easier said than done.

"We're almost there," Estella spoke softly from behind me. "This will be over soon."

She was trying to reassure me, but I could hear the hitch in her breathing and the shakiness in her voice. The truth was, she had no idea what to expect, but being forced to watch what was coming must have been a living nightmare for her. I wish I could shield her from all of this.

"I can walk," I told the person carrying me. I'd much rather go to my possible death standing on my own two feet.

'We're not going to die. Rylan would never allow it.' My wolf's confidence in our mate was admirable, but I didn't think she fully understood what was about to happen. Hell, I wasn't even sure, but I trusted Faela, and I trusted the Moon Spirit.

The person holding me huffed, let my legs swing free of his arm, and helped steady me as I stood. I didn't know why he was helping me, but I hoped it was a good sign that maybe there was still a part of him that wasn't under Tamra's control.

We walked in silence, and after my shoulder brushed against a stone wall, I realized we were still in the Cage. The path seemed familiar, and I wondered if we were being led to the same place, I'd entered the prison from the first time.

My suspicion was confirmed when the man who'd been carrying me suddenly grabbed me and jumped up out of the hole. Once safely on the ground, I looked around and saw the same boulders that I'd traversed in order to reach the Cage's secret entrance.

It was completely dark, the only light coming from the stars up above, and I realized that there was no moon in the sky. That meant that the Moon Spirit would be at its weakest, and the Shadow Wolf would be the strongest. Tamra had planned everything down to the minute details, it seemed. She was recreating the night she killed her sister.

I turned to Estella, who had clumsily climbed up through the hole with her wolf right behind her. She was visibly shaking, but her chin was lifted, and she looked ready for anything.

"This way," the man who'd been carrying me said, grabbing my bicep and pulling me away from the entrance.

The ambient light from the stars helped my wolf eyes to focus on my surroundings. The first thing I noticed once they adjusted was that the man who had a hold on me was Bear. The alpha of my old pack and Tamra's mate.

He didn't seem to recognize me at all. He just stared straight ahead and carried out his duty like it was normal. Seeing him completely under Tamra's control, knowing that he had been her first victim, made me furious. She'd taken away his free will, giving him no choice in his life. I couldn't imagine being forced to marry another after finding your true mate.

"Over here, love," Tamra called, waving to him beside a large free-standing stone.

"Bear, you don't have to do this." I tried reasoning with the shifter, but he ignored me, giving no indication that he had heard a word I said.

Bear didn't react, just led me over to where Tamra stood. Pushing my back against the stone, he held me still while she tied my hands together then lifted them above my head. She quickly restrained the rest of my body. Jerking and protesting did absolutely nothing against the alpha's hold.

I relaxed, needing to conserve my energy for whatever was about to happen.

Estella and her wolf were tied up next to me with three shifters surrounding her. One was in his wolf form, and Estella's white wolf growled a warning, putting herself between it and her human.

"Bear, please." I tried again to reason with my mate's uncle, but he just looked at me blankly, like he had no idea who I was.

Tamra reappeared in my field of vision, handing him the ends of the ropes that restrained me.

"I wouldn't try to struggle," she said conversationally, drawing closer until she was about a foot away from me. "Bear will be behind you, keeping you secure. I have no doubt you're strong, but he and the darkness are much stronger. They'll rip you in half before you can escape."

I lifted my chin and met her eyes, letting her know that I wasn't afraid of her. She could restrain me all she wanted, belittle me even, but I would not give her the satisfaction of cowering.

"I like your backbone." Tamra stepped back to look me up and down. "Any other time, I would enjoy breaking you, but unfortunately, we don't have time. We need to start soon so I can watch your mate go insane as I kill you."

My jaw flexed, and my hands curled into fists above my head. My lip twitched with the need to bare my teeth. I knew without a shadow of doubt that Rylan was on his way, and he wouldn't let her hurt me. He would set the world ablaze. She should be scared of the monster Rylan could be. Underestimating him would be her downfall.

Suddenly, howls filled the air, hundreds of them making my chest clench. We were surrounded by hundreds of wolves, all waiting patiently. Answering howls sounded from the distance, a much smaller number in comparison, which made my heart sink. Rylan and our pack were outnumbered, and I had no way to warn him that he was running into a trap.

Fear raced down my spine, and I reached for the bond, ready to do just about anything in order to get through to him.

'Rylan! Rylan, it's a trap!' I yelled through our bond, desperately hoping that my words would get through.

I felt a stirring on the other end then nothing. Biting my lip, I wondered if I could howl and alert them all. Glancing at Estella, I tried to silently tell her what I was about to do. Her eyes narrowed, but that was it. It was probably the best I was going to get.

As quietly as possible, I sucked in the deepest breath I could muster while my wolf pushed forward, ready to use both our voices to get our message to our mate. My head tilted back, my throat opened, and my diaphragm tensed.

I howled, the sound breaking the overwhelming silence. It sounded like two different voices, when it was actually just one. I sent a silent prayer to the Moon Spirit, hoping that Rylan would hear me.

My eyes closed, and my head tilted back, so I didn't see the fist shooting toward my neck. Pain exploded from my throat, cutting off my howl. I felt a crunch that made my head reel. I tried to draw in breath to scream, but I couldn't. The trauma from the blow had cut off my voice and my air flow. I choked and tried to cough, my lungs screaming for oxygen.

My wolf healing kicked in, allowing me to suck in a tiny breath before stars appeared and my vision became hazy.

A howl split the air, making me jump. Through the blur of pain, I saw Estella's wolf continuing the howl that I started. The wolves surrounding her surged, but the human Estella kicked out and managed to trip them up, allowing her wolf to finish the howl.

"It doesn't matter." Tamra waved away the shifters Estella had tripped. "It's too late for them. They'll never get here in time to save you."

Turning back to me, she raised a long and shockingly white dagger. My heart started beating faster as I registered that I was staring at the blade Rylan had nearly decapitated me with.

Tamra stepped toward me, the dagger in her hand gleaming with an eerie white glow, like it was made of moonlight instead of steel.

"I'm sure you recognize this," she whispered, tapping the point on my neck where the blade had been lodged after the Gala. "This is a unique blade that the darkness made for me. You see, it's not metal." She moved the tip to my left collarbone, and I swallowed past the panic, determined not to let it show. "It's actually bone. Her bone in fact." Tamra's eyes flitted sideways to her sister. "The darkness took the Moon Spirit power from my sister's body, forged this blade, and gifted it to me. A thank you for bringing him into this world."

187

The shadows surrounding us moved, drawing closer to her as she explained the dagger in her hand.

"Wolves are not bothered by silver like the stories say, but the bones of the dead frighten even the strongest alpha. Do you know why?"

I shook my head, having no clue why the bones of shifters could hurt us.

"Because darkness deals in death. Bones are a testament to that. Shifter bones do not belong to the Moon Spirit. They belong to the dark."

The blade nicked my collarbone again, but this time I felt the cool bite followed by the warm trickle of blood that flowed from the wound.

Darkness swirled in Tamra's eyes, and she welcomed it like she knew it intimately. A presence swept over me, making my stomach churn violently. The shadows coalesced behind her until a completely black wolf appeared. It was taller than any wolf I had ever seen, nearly a head above Tamra's.

"It's time," the enormous wolf said, speaking out loud for everyone to hear.

Tamra trembled, not in terror but more in rapture. The voice of her master caused a physical reaction from her. It was grotesque, and I fought the urge to gag. This whole thing was messed up, and I couldn't understand how she didn't see it.

'She only sees what she wants to see,' my wolf said, a vague sense of pity for her flitting across my mind.

Tamra bit her lower lip then lifted the bone blade above my head. At first, I thought she was going to cut through my bonds, but that was wishful thinking on my part. The quick slices on my wrist were almost painless. Blood poured down my arms, the liquid covering the filagree marks. A whimper escaped when the blade moved down to my throat.

"No," Estella yelled, as her wolf snarled pulling on her restraints.

That's enough, Tamra. A soft voice drifted through all of our thoughts. *I'm here. Let my Alpha Seeker be.*

I couldn't help the gasp that escaped when I saw the all-white wolf standing a couple paces behind Tamra and the Shadow Wolf.

My heart ached when I saw the Moon Spirit, knowing what it was about to do in order to save me. I wanted to yell, to beg the wolf not to sacrifice itself for my life but also knowing that it wouldn't listen. All of Faela and its careful planning all led to this exact moment.

"Excellent." The Shadow Wolf panted with excitement. "Time to die."

The dark wolf lunged, but before it could take two steps, a sound reached our ears. It was deep and rumbly. It shook the ground beneath our feet, followed by a wave of power that knocked nearly every wolf to their knees.

With my heart pounding in my ears, my eyes narrowed on the tree line directly across from me. An enormous figure darted out. At first glance, I'd say it was a monster, but after further inspection, I recognized it for who it was.

Rylan!

Chapter Twenty-Nine

Rylan

My mate was tied to a fucking tree. She looked like a sacrifice, with blood covering her arms and soaking her clothes. Fury coated my insides, making it impossible to control the angry beast inside of me.

Fur rippled over my skin as my body shifted. Bones cracked and rearranged themselves, followed by flesh and sinew stretching and constricting. It felt like I was being skinned alive, but I ignored the pain. Nothing would distract me from the sight of my mate bound and tied like some animal.

My earlier roar had freed a good number of wolves from Tamra's hold, but I knew that it wasn't nearly enough. I'd been driving on pure instinct ever since Pearl had been taken. I needed a level head, which I'd managed for the most part until I laid eyes on her again. Seeing her covered in blood and helpless to save herself caused something inside me to snap.

I shoved my pack to the side, letting the change from man to beast take over. Heedless of the danger I was no doubt running into, I sprinted forward, exiting the trees in a matter of seconds. My form continued to grow as I ran, my legs eating up the distance as molten fury flowed through my veins, scorching a trail throughout my body until all I could see, think, and smell was my mate's blood.

I would fucking kill every last one of them for daring to touch my mate.

When I was twenty feet away, several things happened all at once. Tamra whirled around with a glowing dagger in her hand that I immediately recognized. Her eyes met mine, and I saw absolute hatred and hunger directed fully at me.

I'd heard Pearl's then Estella's howl. I'd heard the warning, knew it was a trap, but I didn't care. I released enough wolves and added them to my pack for the odds to even out. Which freed me to save my mate.

Nothing else mattered except freeing my mate and getting her the hell out of here.

"Rylan," Pearl screamed while Estella yelled out a warning, but it was too late.

Tamra's arm swung back; the handle of the dagger gripped in her palm. A small smile pulled at the corner of her mouth as the blade left her hand. The big wolf shadow disappeared, but I would deal with it later.

I watched in slow motion as the dagger that nearly decapitated my mate somersaulted through the air, aimed right for my heart. My wolf pulled back, but our forward momentum meant that it was too late. There was no way we'd be able to move in time.

A white blur appeared out of nowhere. I opened my mouth to yell, but it jumped in front of the dagger that glowed with a strange white light. At first, I thought it was Estella's wolf, but I knew that she wouldn't leave her human half unguarded. If I was her wolf, that was exactly what I would do.

There was only one other white wolf that it could be.

The Moon Spirit had jumped between me and the dagger. I watched as it stabbed the white wolf in its tender underbelly.

"No," I gasped out, too stunned to react to what I was witnessing.

That moment of disbelief, that moment of hesitation, was how everything went to shit. The dagger didn't stop; it went straight through the Moon Spirit. My wolf and I put everything into backpedaling, but it was too late.

The dagger was cold as it sliced into my shoulder. I wasn't sure what I expected, but it wasn't an ice-cold bite, followed by agony so intense I blacked out for a second.

I fell to the ground, and Pearl screamed as she pulled fruitlessly against her binds. Somehow, I shifted back to my human form by the time I hit the dirt. I looked down at my chest, saw the blood coating my torso and the dagger sticking out of my shoulder.

My vision tunneled, my heartbeat pounding loudly in my ears drowning out all of the other noise. I grabbed the handle of the dagger and ripped the blade out of my body. There was no pain, only the warm gush of blood that slushed out of the wound. I could feel my soul leaving my body and I wondered if Pearl had felt like this back at the Gala. A cool detachment calmed my mind as my heart slowed to a beat that was dangerously close to stopping.

I blinked, my eyes seeking out Pearl's, wanting her to be the last thing I saw before I closed them for the final time. Her hair was floating around her perfect face, her arm glowing with a light so bright it hurt to look at her, but I forced my eyes to remain where they were. I watched in fascination as she screamed, her brown eyes lightening until they glowed bright white too.

Movement beside her drew my attention. I sucked in a breath, watching as Tamra stood next to my mate, a sadistic grin on her face. I tried to yell a warning but knew there was no time. Without thinking, I tossed the dagger in my hand, catching the tip in my palm as it came down. With the last of my strength and breath, I hurled the blade toward my aunt. Spending the final moments on this earth saving my mate.

But a shadow appeared between Tamra and my throw. I thought for sure that the Shadow Wolf had blocked my strike, but I was too weak to keep watching.

I just hoped that my actions had saved Pearl from dying. Something was definitely happening to her, but I knew that she was strong and would be all right.

Darkness closed in around me, feeling like a friend I hadn't seen in a long time. A flash of white seared my retinas through my eyelids, and then I fell into an endless sky full of stars strangely without moon.

Chapter Thirty

P earl

Everything burned.

Moon Forged

the third book in the Alpha Seeker Series is available for preorder!

Preorder Moon Forged Here

ALPHA SEEKER

BOOK THREE: MOON FORGED
LELA GRAYCE

About the Author

Lela Grayce lives in rural Wyoming in a small college town. She is married to her best friend and hero. By day she is a working mom and wife but by night she is lost in dreams, moonlight, and delusions that she is, in fact, Batman.

You can connect with me on:
- https://lelagrayce.com
- https://www.facebook.com/LelaGrayce

Subscribe to my newsletter:
- https://www.subscribepage.com/lelagrayce2023

Also by Lela Grayce

Ashes of Blood: Dragon Mafia Chronicles Book One
Do not serve drinks to a dragon mob boss. They bite. Zero stars. Do not recommend.

Blood Arrow: The Forest Hood Series Book One
There's safety in the forest.

Arrow of Loxley isn't the simpering lady of court she pretends to be.

Witch's Fancy: Watchers and Artifacts

Book One

Despite owning a magic shop, having to play it safe by keeping a low profile on her talents has caused Fancy's life to fall short of the mystical adventure she hoped for. Until a detective from the Nightwatch sauntered in. Detective Walker is as hot as they come and has a powerful need... for Fancy's unique abilities.

Areion (Lunar Medallion Series Book One)

Turning eighteen is the highlight of every teenager's life. Or at least it is for Wendy and her twin sister DeeDee. When their adoptive parents gift them with medallions belonging to their late mother, they have no idea their lives are about to change.

Printed in Great Britain
by Amazon